THE HOCKEY SWEATER
AND OTHER STORIES

NOVELS BY ROCH CARRIER
IN TRANSLATION BY SHEILA FISCHMAN
AVAILABLE FROM ANANSI

La Guerre, Yes Sir! (1970)
Floralie, Where Are You? (1971)
Lady With Chains (1991)

THE
HOCKEY
SWEATER

AND OTHER STORIES

ROCH CARRIER

TRANSLATED BY
SHEILA FISCHMAN

First published in French in 1979 as *Les Enfants du bonhomme dans la lune*.
First published in English in 1979 by House of Anansi Press Ltd.

This edition published in 2012 by House of Anansi Press Inc.
www.houseofanansi.com

House of Anansi Press is committed to protecting our natural environment. This book is made
of material from well-managed FSC®-certified forests and other controlled sources.

House of Anansi Press is a Global Certified Accessible™ (GCA by Benetech) publisher. The
ebook version of this book meets stringent accessibility standards and is available to students and
readers with print disabilities.

25 24 23 22 21   2 3 4 5 6

Library and Archives Canada Cataloguing in Publication

Carrier, Roch, 1937–
[Enfants du bonhomme dans la lune. English]
The hockey sweater and other stories / Roch Carrier ; translated
by Sheila Fischman ; introduction by Dave Bidini.

Translation of: Les enfants du bonhomme dans la lune.
Issued also in electronic format.
ISBN 978-1-77089-251-4

I. Fischman, Sheila II. Title. III. Title: Enfants du bonhomme
dans la lune. English.

ps8505.a77e5413 2012   c843'.54   c2012-903569-6

Library of Congress Control Number: 2012939827

Cover design: Brian Morgan
Cover illustration: Genevieve Simms
Typesetting: Marijke Friesen

*House of Anansi Press respectfully acknowledges that the land on which we operate is the Traditional
Territory of many Nations, including the Anishinabeg, the Wendat, and the Haudenosaunee. It is also the
Treaty Lands of the Mississaugas of the Credit.*

*We acknowledge for their financial support of our publishing program the Canada Council for the Arts,
the Ontario Arts Council, and the Government of Canada We acknowledge the financial support of the
Government of Canada through the National Translation Program for Book Publishing, an initiative of the
Action Plan for Official Languages — 2018–2023: Investing in Our Future, for our translation activities.*

Printed and bound in Canada

INTRODUCTION
by DAVE BIDINI

ONCE, DURING A WEDDING, a friend and I drew up a list: WORST PEOPLE IN HISTORY. It was a game we borrowed from Roger Kahn in *The Boys of Summer*. We wrote our versions on monogrammed napkins and passed them across the table through a jumble of biscuit plates and half-full wine glasses. He read mine, I read his. And then we shook our heads and laughed. At the top of my list, I'd written two obvious names: Hitler and Stalin. Stalin, for a moment, had been crossed out and replaced with Genghis Khan, but I reconsidered. My friend's list was the same, only before he'd crossed out Stalin, then uncrossed it, he'd written Mrs. Francis, our grade six teacher who had a face like a shovel and breath like whatever happens to be stuck to your boot. "Mrs. Francis really hated you," I told him. "But she didn't hate everyone. I actually think she liked me. Was fond of me. Which always made me a little suspicious of my character." My friend nodded. "One way or another, she scarred every kid she ever crossed," he said. "Still, her reign of terror was limited to one side of the hemisphere, while Stalin had more of a world view. That's why he made it and not her."

"Fair enough," I said. "Should we even discuss our third choice?"

"That would distinguish it somehow," he said. "And in no way am I doing that."

He had a point. The third name we'd written on our respective WORST PEOPLE IN HISTORY napkins was the Montreal Canadiens. Neither of us named an actual player or coach or goon or goaltender. Instead, we used the collective term, because, to us, the Montreal Canadiens were and are a collective evil, beating out Pol Pot and Carrot Top. Our hatred of the team, the organization, the arena, the city, the ticket takers, the popcorn technicians was such that we never even called them by their prosaic nickname: the Habs. Neither did we support bands, poets, actors or heads of state who'd ever cheered for the Montreal Canadiens. This is why all Viggo Mortensen films will be forever flawed and why, after being forced by friends to walk the Main, Schwartz's treasured and delicious smoked meat sits in a sad lump on my plate.

There is one exception to this cultural and sporting absolute. To find out what it is, all you have to do is look at the front of this book. For us, and for many Hab-nots, "The Hockey Sweater" was free of our prejudice. Just as the work of James Baldwin might have inspired the American Civil Rights movement, or Stud Terkel's *The Great War* changed the way we perceived military conflict, Roch Carrier managed to bring Canadiens and Leafs fans together with "The Hockey Sweater" — among the greatest of all literary feats, and the result, I think, of the author pleasantly and affectionately lampooning both teams and their sensitive, territorial supporters. That *The Hockey Sweater and Other Stories* has been around for so long ensured that the warmth of its prose got to us early. Of all the books I read — or was read — as a kid, I remember *The Hockey Sweater and Other Stories* as much as I remember *Tarzan: King of the Jungle* or *When Dinosaurs Walked the Earth*. Only, unlike those books, *The Hockey Sweater and Other*

Stories takes place here. In Canada. In the winter. That's you and I out on the pond, shkkking and shkkking on bent ankles across the ragged crust.

It also helps that *The Hockey Sweater and Other Stories* is hilarious: a forebear of *King Leary* (the novel) as well as *Goon* and *Perfectly Normal* (the movies). It's only recently that our culture has discovered hockey as a setting rich and appropriate enough for art — see *Hockey Night in Canada*'s musical openings and HBO's gorgeous 24/7 documentary series — but Roch Carrier was light years ahead of this. "The Hockey Sweater" is also the ultimate Canadian coming-of-age story, and one based on the author's experiences growing up in small town Quebec. Our protagonist — the young Carrier — finds himself suffering the wrath and outrage of parents, peers and prefects, each for different reasons, but mostly because of having worn a Toronto Maple Leafs sweater to play shinny with his friends, all of them devoted to the Montreal Canadiens and their '50s star, Maurice "The Rocket" Richard. Many have tried to divine the message behind this legendary — as well as short and perfectly built — book, but to view it coldly and in strictly moral terms grounds the flight of the narrative and slows its infectious energy. "The Hockey Sweater," really, is about embracing life no matter what the circumstances, which, in a land of cold and winter, is as good a lesson as any.

Above all, "The Hockey Sweater" addresses the disparity of Canadian life and manages to celebrate it. Because I am loath to admit it — ever — I'm glad that Roch Carrier had the courage to say what so many of us cannot: that, without the Montreal Canadiens, the Toronto Maple Leafs wouldn't exist, and vice versa. It's an unspoken but universal truth among fans that no team can exist in a vacuum. Otherwise, we're playing ourselves, and where's the fun in that?

A few years ago, I had the chance to return to my own favourite small hockey town, Mercuria Cuic in Transylvania. One evening, I presented a "Hockey Film Night" in the local town hall, and, to my astonishment and delight, the entire village showed up. People stood outside and watched through the windows; others teemed over the balconies to view the small screen we'd set up near the front of the room. One of the first things I showed them was a clip from the animated NFB film based on Carrier's book. Through a translator, I explained the story as best I could, focusing on the Leafs-Canadiens rivalry as a way of comparing Cuic's rivalry with Steaua, the big money Romanian team. When I told the crowd about how the young Carrier was forced to wear a Leafs sweater — "Could you imagine a young boy walking around town in a Steaua sweater?" — they gasped. As I screened the clip, I thought they expected to find something very dark and serious, but, within moments, Carrier's unmistakable voice filled the room while colours splashed across the screen. Soon there was a giggle or two, and then bursts of laugher. Outside, the snow fell lightly on the cold ground.

Suddenly, everywhere, it was winter.

CONTENTS

THE NUN WHO RETURNED
TO IRELAND

AFTER MY FIRST day of school I ran back to the house, holding out my reader.

"Mama, I learned how to read!" I announced.

"This is an important day," she replied; "I want your father to be here to see."

We waited for him. I waited as I'd never waited before. And as soon as his step rang out on the floor of the gallery, my first reader was open on my knees and my finger was pointing to the first letter in a short sentence.

"Your son learned to read today," my mother declared through the screen door. She was as excited as I.

"Well, well!" said my father. "Things happen fast nowadays. Pretty soon, son, you'll be able to do like me — read the newspaper upside down in your sleep!"

"Listen to me!" I said.

And I read the sentence I'd learned in school that day, from Sister Brigitte. But instead of picking me up and lifting me in his arms, my father looked at my mother and my mother didn't come and kiss her little boy who'd learned to read so quickly.

"What's going on here?" my father asked.

"I'd say it sounds like English," said my mother. "Show me your book." (She read the sentence I'd learned to decipher.) "I'd say you're reading as if you were English. Start again."

I reread the short sentence.

"You're reading with an English accent!" my mother exclaimed.

"I'm reading the way Sister Brigitte taught me."

"Don't tell me he's learning his own mother tongue in English," my father protested.

I had noticed that Sister Brigitte didn't speak the way we did, but that was quite natural because we all knew that nuns don't do anything the way other people do: they didn't dress like everybody else, they didn't get married, they didn't have children and they always lived in hiding. But as far as knowing whether Sister Brigitte had an English accent, how could I? I'd never heard a single word of English.

Over the next few days I learned that she hadn't been born in our village; it seemed very strange that someone could live in the village without being born there, because everyone else in the village had been born in the village.

Our parents weren't very pleased that their children were learning to read their mother tongue with an English accent. In whispers, they started to say that Sister Brigitte was Irish — that she hadn't even been born in Canada. Monsieur Cassidy, the undertaker, was Irish too, but he'd been born in the village, while Sister Brigitte had come from Ireland.

"Where's Ireland?" I asked my mother.

"It's a very small, very green little country in the ocean, far, far away."

As our reading lessons proceeded I took pains to pronounce the vowels as Sister Brigitte did, to emphasize the same syllables as she; I was so impatient to read the books my uncles brought back from their far-off colleges. Suddenly it was important for me to know.

"Sister Brigitte, where's Ireland?"

She put down her book.

"Ireland is the country where my parents were born, and my grandparents and my great-grandparents. And I was born in Ireland too. I was a little girl in Ireland. When I was a child like you I lived in Ireland. We had horses and sheep. Then the Lord asked me to become his servant . . ."

"What does that mean?"

"The Lord asked me if I wanted to become a nun. I said yes. So then I left my family and I forgot Ireland and my village."

"Forgot your village?"

I could see in her eyes that she didn't want to answer my question.

"Ever since, I've been teaching young children. Some of the children who were your age when I taught them are grandparents now, old grandparents."

Sister Brigitte's face, surrounded by her starched coif, had no age; I learned that she was old, very old, because she had been a teacher to grandparents.

"Have you ever gone back to Ireland?"

"God didn't want to send me back."

"You must miss your country."

"God asked me to teach little children to read and write so every child could read the great book of life."

"Sister Brigitte, you're older than our grandparents! Will you go back to Ireland before you die?"

The old nun must have known from my expression that death was so remote for me I could speak of it quite innocently, as I would speak of the grass or the sky. She said simply:

"Let's go on with our reading. School children in Ireland aren't as disorderly as you."

All that autumn we applied ourselves to our reading; by December we could read the brief texts Sister Brigitte wrote on the blackboard herself, in a pious script we tried awkwardly to imitate; in every text the word Ireland always appeared. It was by writing the word Ireland that I learned to form a capital I.

After Christmas holidays Sister Brigitte wasn't at the class-room door to greet us; she was sick. From our parents' whispers we learned that Sister Brigitte had lost her memory. We weren't surprised. We knew that old people always lose their memories and Sister Brigitte was an old person because she had been a teacher to grandparents.

Late in January, the nuns in the convent discovered that Sister Brigitte had left her room. They looked everywhere for her, in all the rooms and all the classrooms. Outside, a storm was blow-ing gusts of snow and wind; you couldn't see Heaven or earth, as they said. Sister Brigitte, who had spent the last few weeks in her bed, had fled into the storm. Some men from the village spotted her black form in the blizzard: beneath her vast mantle she was barefoot. When the men asked her where she was going, Sister Brigitte replied in English that she was going home, to Ireland.

THE SHOEMAKER

BEFORE WE BOUGHT our house it had belonged to a shoemaker who died in it when he was very old. My mother described him to us: short and bent over because he'd spent his whole life stitching leather. The little shoemaker limped: he had a clubfoot and one leg was shorter than the other. He made his own shoes because he wouldn't have been able to find in any store the small, thick-soled boot shaped like a horse's hoof for his crippled foot.

There was a very low attic on the top of the lean-to attached to our house. That was where our mother used to store boxes of clothing that would be worn by the other children when they arrived. She would let us climb up the stepladder with her. With our heads jutting through the opening in the ceiling, our glances would fall on boxes, suitcases, old magazines, framed photographs — things in the attic which, in the beam of the flashlight, seemed to be whispering secrets. Perched on the stepladder, with my head in a trapdoor which was scarcely higher than the attic floor, I would ascend into a dream from which my mother had to snatch me away. Climbing down the stepladder, I would always return from it a little dazed. In one corner of the attic was a pile of the shoemaker's tools. They didn't belong to us. The tools were waiting as though the shoemaker would come back and use them: rolled-up strips of leather, shoes to which he hadn't had time to attach the soles, spindles of thread, punches, an awl, a currier's beam with long wooden tongs that held the leather as he sewed it, a tripod, shoemaker's knives. My mother explained what all the tools were used for, but she didn't touch them. Often at night, before I fell asleep, I thought about the little shoemaker with the clubfoot who had lived in our house and died there, and whose tools were still waiting for him.

In those days we knew that man dies only to be reborn. There was absolutely no doubt in my mind that if the little shoemaker's tools were still in our attic — and his leather and his thread — he would come back to carry on his trade. The roof cracked, a nail creaked in the wood: in my bed I knew that the little shoemaker had returned. I burrowed deep in the mattress and pulled the sheet over my head. I fell asleep.

One morning I saw my shoes by the bed, with brand new soles made of fine, shiny leather; the worn-down heels had been replaced; my shoes were new again.

"Who did that?" I cried as I ran down the stairs. "My shoes look even nicer than when they were new!"

"Your shoes were so worn-out it was a disgrace," said my mother, who was feeding my little brother from a spoon. "Last night while you were asleep I took them to the new shoemaker."

I went back up to my room, suspecting my mother hadn't told me the truth. There are so many things that parents don't want to tell children, so many things they refused to explain to me, so many things I couldn't understand till I was grown up. This time, though, I guessed. I knew, even though my mother hadn't wanted to tell me the truth. During the night my shoes had been repaired by the little shoemaker with the clubfoot!

I left for school earlier than usual. There was something in our village more important than the sun shining down on us:

my shoes. Their gleam was more dazzling than the September morning. I didn't walk to school, nor did I run: I flew. My new soles, sewn on by the little shoemaker with the clubfoot who had come back to earth at night to ply his trade in our house, didn't really rest on the ground the way cows' feet did, or horses', or my schoolmates': they made me fly, though I still looked like someone who was walking. I knew, though, that I was flying. I had been initiated into one of the great mysteries that dwell in the night. I knew that the little shoemaker with the clubfoot had come, I'd heard him limp, heard him pick up his tools and put them down in the attic.

Everyone at our school wore shoes. The nuns wouldn't have tolerated a barefoot student and no mother would dare send a barefoot child to the village school. In the schools on the concession roads more than a mile from the village, little schools built beside the dusty gravel roads, many of the children didn't wear shoes, but we who went to the village school proudly wore shoes. It wasn't until after school that the children of large families would take their shoes off so as not to wear them out too much.

When I arrived in the schoolyard the others immediately noticed my shoes. My classmates came closer to look at them. I went to stand against the big willow, the boys' meeting place, to show them off.

"You got new shoes!"

"Lucky you."

"I have to wear my brother's shoes when they get too small for him, but when they're too small for him they're too worn out for me."

I began to explain, sitting on the books I carried in a canvas bag.

"These aren't new shoes. They're my old ones. While I was asleep . . ."

And I told my schoolmates, sitting on their books like me, how my shoes had been rebuilt in the night by the little shoemaker with the clubfoot who used to live in our house before he died, and whose tools were still there.

A harsh laugh struck me like a slap in the face, interrupting my story; one of the big boys had come over to listen to me and he was laughing, holding his stomach.

"Listen to him! Did the atomic bomb land on your head?"

A few days earlier the Americans had dropped an atomic bomb on Hiroshima and it had burned alive thousands of women, men and children.

We heard about it on the radio, *L'Action catholique* had probably written something about it on the front page and my parents had most likely talked about the article in *L'Action catholique* — but I have to admit that I don't remember Hiroshima.

I searched through my memory, trying to find that childhood day, the way you search page by page, paragraph by paragraph, for a passage in a book you've already read. But instead of recalling something that burned so brightly it could have set fire to a corner of my memory, painfully, all I could remember of that autumn day was the little shoemaker with the clubfoot.

That gap in my recollections still irritates me, but a man likely doesn't choose what will come to haunt his memory.

In the next life, when the people of Hiroshima remember this earth, they will see again the bright explosion that wrenched their bodies from their souls. But I wish they could remember instead a little shoemaker with a clubfoot who, as they were sleeping, came and mended shoes worn out from having played too much on the earth covered with dandelions and daisies.

IDIOT DEATH

IDIOT DEATH

SOMETIMES AS HE was dunking a cookie in his tea, my father would announce:

"Tomorrow, son, you're coming with me; it'll do you good to see something of life."

The next day we would set off in his black Ford and behind us the village, like a hat on the mountaintop, was erased in the dust of the gravel road. We drove down roads where, often, there wasn't even any dust because they were dirt roads and always damp. The car advanced slowly, its belly getting caught in the ruts, while along the road from time to time a frame house turned grey by time would appear in a space chewed out of the dense forest: a flock of children would burst out and come running to watch us pass. These children of all ages, barefoot, wore clothes too big for them, that looked to me like sacks. My father said:

"The good Lord, he's fair, but he didn't make everybody rich."

After giving me a few moments' silence to think about this he added:

"Duplessis hasn't even given them electricity."

For me, this meant that in the evening all the children would do their homework around the same table, lit by a single oil lamp:

so many children around a single table on which, earlier, they had eaten a porridge, which was what I'd been told poor people ate. Often, my father would stop and go into the house to talk with the father. The children would approach our car and come and look at me. I didn't like the way they smelled of the stable. Often they'd invite me to get out so they could show me a car they'd built out of old wheels, and they'd show me tame animals — snakes, a squirrel, an owl. When I came back to the village my head would be buzzing.

That day, my father stopped before one of the unpainted houses. A man was sitting on the steps in front of the door. There were no children around. They must have been in the fields, picking raspberries. I decided to wait in the car.

"Bonjour, Philémon!" said my father.

"Salut, Georges, haven't seen you around for a while."

"Is it you that's missing me, Philémon — or your wife?"

A form appeared in the screenless doorway and Philémon's wife called out, before going back into the shadows:

"You're a pair of skunks, you two!"

"Your wife expecting again?" my father asked with a mocking smile.

"This'll make fourteen, Georges," said Philémon, his satisfaction stretching into a grin. "How about you? Not up to making fourteen, eh?"

The shrill sound of a crying child came from the house.

"Philémon," my father asked, "is that howl telling us your fourteenth's arrived?"

"If it is, Georges, I better get to work on the fifteenth right away!"

His wife, her form blending with the shadows, reappeared in the doorway.

"I'd just as soon the children didn't hear when the two of you get together."

I was in the car, listening; the words were familiar words, but they were speaking a language I didn't know. I understood nothing of what they said. I was careful to laugh at their jokes when they did, for it was important that I seem to understand.

"What you got up your sleeve for me today, Philémon?"

"Today, Georges, I'm cleaning my gun. Something wrong with your eyes?"

In fact the man was holding a rifle across his knees, rubbing the barrel with a rag.

"I like a gun that's as clean as my eyeballs," said the man. "Don't look. It's as bright as an electric light."

As he spoke the man had taken the rifle from his knees and was pointing it in my father's direction.

"Watch out, Philémon," said my father, "you're gonna scare me. That's no rosary you got in your hands, it's a gun."

My father took a few steps back, towards the car.

"Come on now, Georges, don't be scared. You know very well . . ."

"Philémon, that thing scares me."

Laughing, the man pointed the rifle at my father; with his left eye shut, he aimed.

"If you was a deer now, Georges, you'd be out of luck today. Ha ha!"

"Philémon!" my father ordered curtly, "put that down. Maybe it's loaded!"

"Come on, Georges, I ain't crazy; if my gun was loaded I wouldn't be playing with it."

The man aimed at my father, but the rifle moved. The man's shoulders shook because he was laughing so hard at the sight of my terrified father. My father did his utmost to get away.

"I can't run, Philémon. My legs won't move."

My father fell to his knees. The rifle was levelled at him.

"If you was a deer, Georges, I could pick your forehead or the nose or even the heart. Or maybe . . . Ha ha!"

His words were shaken by the laughter gurgling from his mouth. The rifle pursued my father. He had folded his hands as he did when he prayed, and in the car I had my hands folded, too.

"Philémon," my father said, weeping, "I pray the good Lord not to let you shoot."

The man still stalked my father through the sight.

"Georges, I'd'a never thought you'd be scared of a gun, like a little girl."

The man was laughing harder and harder; he was stamping his feet in their big boots with pleasure, while I was trying to slip down on the seat so I couldn't see anything. I was as paralysed as my father.

"Philémon, I don't want my boy to see me die."

My father had let himself drop to the ground, his face in his arms. The man had stopped laughing — rather, he was shouting with pleasure, or coughing or spitting. He was so delighted he couldn't hold the rifle; he put it back on his knees so he could wipe the tears and saliva with the back of his big brown hands. Slowly, he was calming down. My father didn't move. I looked at him lying on the ground, I could see his white calves between his trousers and his socks, I could see the worn-down heels of his shoes. The man was no longer laughing. He came towards my father. His big belly sagged and he was dragging his boots. He tapped my father's head with the barrel of the rifle.

"No," my father shouted, "no, NO."

"Georges," said the man, "of all the people that's come this way, nobody's ever made me laugh as much as you. You know very well this gun ain't loaded. Look!"

He pointed the weapon towards the sky. The sky thundered as it had never done during the severe storms that froze us with fear some nights. The rifle jumped to the ground.

"I killed him!" the man shouted. "I killed Georges! I killed him!"

He was weeping. Slowly, my father got up, shaking the grass off his suit.

"I killed Georges!" the man cried.

In the doorway, the shadow of his wife said nothing. The man kept shouting:

"I killed him! I killed him!"

My father bent over, picked up the rifle and held it out to the man.

"Philémon, don't be so scared."

And to me he said:

"Come here, son, this is gonna be a lot finer day than I thought."

I'm the same age now as my father was at the time of the great fright. If I find myself thinking about death I can't help seeing it as I perceived it that day: idiotic. It doesn't know that it can kill.

THE MACHINE FOR DETECTING EVERYTHING THAT'S AMERICAN

AT THE FOOT of the mountain two or three streams wound their way through the alders. The water was very clear. In it we could see minnows, select the ones we wanted, watch them bite the hook. It was impossible to come home empty-handed.

In the spring as soon as the snow had gone, the Americans were back, as we used to say, with cars bigger than the curé's to which were attached marvellous motorboats. The Americans had come to fish. With their big boats they didn't venture into our three little streams; no, they went farther, into the mountains, to fish in a lake that belonged to them. Because the Americans came from so far away to fish in their lake, the trout in it were longer than in any lake in the United States. Of that we were absolutely sure.

There was no end to the magnificent boats, the cars with licences bearing names like magic words and the rich gentlemen who smoked big cigars; they drove through our village as though it wasn't even there. The Americans were in a hurry, as the men in the village said, "to go fishing for trout with a shovel."

I had an inspiration that I confided to my friend Lapin: we didn't have to be satisfied with our grey minnows. We should be more ambitious. We should go fishing in the Americans' lake.

"We aren't allowed," he said. "That lake belongs to the Americans. But the trout are as long as that," my friend the shrewd fisherman sighed.

We went to get our fish nets. Lapin filled his pockets with worms and we stood by the side of the road, waiting for a car that was going towards the Americans' lake. An hour later, Onésime's old truck had taken us to the entrance of the Americans' lake. On the fence was written: DÉFENCE DE PÊCHÉ; NO FISHING. We climbed over, then followed the road to the lake, a road broad enough for the big cars, a road that was better built than our country roads. The lake was as beautiful as the ones on calendars. It was deserted. There was no American fishing from his big motorboat. From our ambush behind a tree, Lapin and I looked all around. Certain we were alone, we walked to the dock where there were a few canoes.

"You know how to paddle?" Lapin asked. "No? Me neither."

"Our fathers weren't Indians, that's for sure."

In a canoe on the Americans' lake we baited our hooks and started to fish. Soon I said to Lapin:

"If we don't stop we'll have to get out of the canoe to make room for the trout."

"Let's scram," said Lapin, "before we get caught."

Back on shore, we threaded our trout through the gills onto slender alder boughs. Then we ran to the road where we began to walk as though we hadn't just come from the Americans' lake. We'd gone scarcely one *arpent* when Onésime came back in his old truck. We ran into the trees with our trout, but he'd seen us and stopped. We had no choice but to get in the truck.

"Nice trout you got there."

"We found them in a little hidden stream," said Lapin.

Onésime knit his thick grey brows, the brows of a man who's seen the world. We looked down, blushing.

"You kids done all right, it's no sin to steal trout from the Americans.... It's just smuggling. You know what that is, smuggling? Don't get caught, children, like some people let themselves. The Code's the Code."

Onésime told us what had happened. Our village was a few miles from the American border where there was a customs station, just a shack. The customs officer only worked during the day. He saw more rabbits than travellers. One man had taken advantage of the night to smuggle across several dozen packages of American cigarettes, with the idea of selling them again in the village. In the morning the customs officer showed up at the smuggler's house and confiscated the cigarettes and even the keys to his car.

"I think," Onésime concluded, "he's going to have to get around on his bicycle for a while. Unless he goes to jail ... Smuggling's a serious thing ... But I wouldn't think they'd hang the man ..."

"How did the customs officer know the man had crossed the border with the cigarettes?"

"The customs officer's got a machine that can detect anything that's American."

Lapin and I said nothing. But we were thinking the same thing. Bringing American cigarettes into the village is a crime, punishable by law; bringing trout you'd fished in the Americans' lake must be the same thing — a crime punishable by law.

Onésime stopped in front of the church.

"Out you get, youngsters, here's where I turn off. Watch out for the Code!"

Lapin stuck the trout under his sweater and we jumped to the sidewalk, looking like butter wouldn't melt in our mouths. With our trout hidden under his sweater, Lapin's chest stuck out as much as Pierrette's. He couldn't walk around with that bump in his sweater for very long. In front of the flowers on Monsieur Rancourt's lawn, my friend Lapin said:

"Let's throw our trout in the flowers."

"No! Somebody'll find them. The customs officer with his machine. And he'll know we put them there."

What were we to do? Lapin sat on the edge of the sidewalk, arms crossed to hide the bump. I did the same. All we could do was think.

"These are our trout. We caught them with our hands and our own worms."

"Yes, but we caught them in the Americans' lake."

"Yes, but that lake's in our country, in our forest."

"Yes, but the lake belongs to the Americans. If we bring something into the village that belongs to the Americans, it's smuggling."

"And with his machine," Lapin concluded, "the customs officer can tell whenever anybody's smuggling."

We were trapped. We ran to the church with our trout. Hidden behind the organ, we waited. We prayed and waited. Would God come to the rescue of two children who, that day, were so fervent? Through the big windows we could see the light grow pale. It was already night in the church, though there was still light on the earth. Would we have to spend the night in hiding? At night the church would be a deep cave, the vigil lights like will-o'-the-wisps. The sacristan began his tour of inspection before locking the church. We would be prisoners till morning.

"The customs officer's machine'll know we're here, but he'll wait till after dark to come and get us."

We didn't want to spend the night in the church. With all the saints and the demons and the damned, the angels and the souls in purgatory, could anyone know what would happen there at night? At night a church could be like Heaven — but it might be like Hell too. Lapin and I had tears in our eyes.

"Our only hope's to confess, admit all our sins . . ."

"And resolve firmly never to sin again," Lapin added.

On tiptoe, silent as angels to escape the sacristan, we emerged from behind the organ, then left the church and ran to the customs officer.

"We brought you some smuggled trout," I said weakly — beaten, guilty.

The customs officer examined them with a knowing eye.

"You didn't clean them . . ."

"We didn't know it was in the Code," my friend Lapin apologized.

"Doesn't matter. Thanks a lot, kids. Matter of fact I was just thinking of some nice trout. Wife! Cook them up in butter. Lots of butter. And garlic too!"

THE DAY I BECAME
AN APOSTATE

I WISH I'D BEEN a bird instead of a child. There are so many countries I could have gone to simply by flapping my wings in the vast blue sky.

I'd have liked so much to go to the moon and visit the nice man whose eyes and mouth you could see on bright nights when the moon is full. But unfortunately we learned in school that I could never go to the moon. The nun explained to us:

"Children, try to imagine if you can, a train that left France in 1608, when Champlain set sail for Quebec; imagine, children, that this train was going eighty miles an hour and never stopping . . . er . . . imagine this train going along a railway that men have built between the earth and the moon; well, children, today this train still wouldn't have reached the moon, whereas Champlain, the founder of Quebec, has been dead for three hundred years. Children, if the good Lord put the moon so far from the earth it's because in His wisdom He didn't want men to go anywhere except on earth."

We remained on the earth, then, and the distant moon seemed like a lamp in the window of the sky. (And yet, in the comic strips in L'Action catholique, men pushed a lever, pressed buttons and rose up to the moon.)

I couldn't go to the moon then, but if I'd been a bird I could certainly have gone to Rome, the Holy City, home of the Pope, the man chosen by God, the only man who never made a mistake, the man to whom God had given the keys to the gates of Heaven. The Pope, the most powerful man in the world, lived in Rome. Once every week he opened his window and made the sign of the cross. Those who saw him perform this act were touched by divine charity and their lives would be filled with goodness and happiness. Rome was bathed in a celestial perfume. But Rome was so far away and I wasn't a bird but a child, condemned to walk in his narrow little shoes on the earth of our village.

Because she was a saint, our nun's Superior had obtained the privilege of going to Rome. There she had experienced the supreme happiness of seeing with her own eyes the Pope — in flesh and blood. Our nun had received a postcard from her Superior. The stamp on it was as beautiful as a diamond. It came from Rome. From the Eternal City. It had come almost from Heaven. And it was as precious as a relic, as a piece of the Pope's own soutane.

"I want that stamp!" I exclaimed.

"Me too!" the other children exclaimed in chorus.

"I can't tear the stamp into thirty-five pieces to please all of you, children; so I'll give it to the one who shows the greatest piety during the holy time of Lent."

I went to mass twice every morning, I said the Rosary as often as twelve times a day. God was pleased with me. He gave the nun the idea that I deserved the stamp from Rome.

IN MID-APRIL the Duplessis government's huge snowplough came to clear the village street. The accumulated snow from the winter was turned over and formed into high cordons on either side of the street. Here and there patches of yellow grass emerged. The snow turned grey. The sky darkened. Spring was hesitating. Spring never dared emerge from winter before the victorious Christ emerged from his grave. The earth was becoming sad because the death of Christ was approaching. The condemnation to death of the Son of God was shameful and the sun refused to shed its light on such a sin. Even the church bells would soon be silent. On Good Friday, in fact, at three o'clock in the afternoon, after Christ's last sigh on the cross, the bells would immediately fly away to Rome to beseech the Pope to forgive the sins committed in the village and ask for his blessing, which they would send out, all year long from the parish steeple on the mountain. The bells left for Rome on the day of Christ's death and returned on Easter to announce his Resurrection.

I think it was an angel who made a suggestion that became more and more pressing; though I had no way to go to the moon it would be very easy for me to go to Rome — with the travelling bells.

The week was interminable. I knew that Good Friday was on the horizon and I was waiting for it, but it came no closer. Each day was longer than the one before. The suffering of Christ was endless. I couldn't pray to him to hasten the arrival of Good Friday . . . I collected the coins I'd hidden in secret places, I wrote a message to put under my pillow, explaining my absence to my parents. Finally, I announced to my friend Lapin that I'd be disappearing for a few days "to a holy city I can't tell you the name of."

"Whereabouts?"

My secret was too big for me.

"I'm going to Rome."

Lapin understood immediately.

"With the bells?"

"That's right."

"Let's both of us go to Rome!"

At last it was Good Friday. In church, my friend Lapin and I followed from prayer to prayer, from psalm to psalm, with extraordinary attentiveness, the last hours of Christ who would die at three o'clock in the afternoon. At that very moment the bells would fly away, taking us with them to Rome. The psalms dragged on, prayers were repeated endlessly, with words that grew longer and longer. The hands on the clock above the pulpit seemed to have stopped moving towards three o'clock.

Much later, it was two minutes to three. Our friends were praying relentlessly and their prayers prevented time from advancing. We wouldn't see our praying friends again until after Easter, after our journey to Rome. Lapin and I waited for Christ's final sigh: perhaps he had decided not to let himself be killed by men that Friday? We waited for three o'clock to arrive in the vestibule — the curé called it the narthex — where the ropes hung down from the bells they were attached to, high up in the steeple. The black hand on the clock suddenly indicated one minute to three. My legs felt wobbly. Soon it would be three o'clock. As it had happened every year since the beginning of the Church, Christ would die at three o'clock and the bells would fly away to Rome. They would transport Lapin and me, clinging to the ropes which we would wind around our waists. As I tied the rope I could feel the bells shudder. They would take flight at precisely three o'clock. Christ on his cross would open his mouth to utter his last word. I could hear his voice, almost dead: *"Sitio!"* He would allow his last sigh to escape. Lapin and I closed our eyes. When we opened them again we would be in Rome.

It was three o'clock. Christ had died. Five past three. Ten. A quarter after three. Christ had been dead for several minutes and we were still clinging to the bell ropes. We were still far from Rome.

"If you ask me," Lapin concluded, "the bells haven't gone anywhere."

I hadn't given up hope: we hadn't gone, but perhaps the bells . . .

"Let's go and look," I suggested.

We untied the ropes and ran up the dark staircase to the rood loft. Perhaps it wasn't too late? From ladder to ladder, from landing to landing, we climbed up the steeple. Breathless, my head heavy with vertigo, at the top of the ladders I came to the little trap door through which I could see — huge, heavy — the bells. Their bronze was not trembling with the desire to fly away. They seemed like great motionless stones. The bells weren't going to Rome. That was the sole truth. Crushing.

My soul was as wounded as my body would have been if it had fallen from the steeple.

"After this," I said, "I can never believe in the Catholic religion again."

The tears in my eyes had not yet dried when I arrived at our house. They'd found the message explaining my departure.

"Back from Rome already, son? Is it a real pretty town?" my father asked, holding back his laughter.

How did I find the strength not to burst out sobbing? I didn't have the strength to accept reality.

"Lapin and I, we went to Rome," I declared, shouting at my incredulous parents.

A few days later they found in the mail a letter decorated with a magnificent stamp from Rome. They recognized my painstaking handwriting immediately. "Rome is the most beautiful city in the whole world."

THE MONTH OF THE DEAD

WHERE ARE THE GHOSTS of yesteryear? Without them we can never know the depth of the night.

Every evening just before sunset, the undertaker used to cross the village slowly, very slowly, in the long black embalmer's car he used to transport the dead to the church and then to the graveyard.

"Looking for your next customer, Monsieur Cassidy?"

"That's what Albert said last year and he isn't with us any more," the undertaker replied.

Monsieur Cassidy, imperturbable, always looked as though he were leading a funeral procession. We didn't dare come close to his car for we were certain this man maintained mysterious relationships beyond the grave. He was a man, we thought, who must be as happy in November as we were in June.

November was the month of the dead. On the second day of the month we little boys and girls, one behind the other in order of height, would follow our teacher, a nun transformed by the wind from the mountain into a bird with broad black wings; her veil and her robe would snap in the cold air and it seemed to us that some malevolent force wanted to pluck her from the earth. We followed her into the graveyard. In no other circumstances would we have dared cross through the iron fence that surrounded it. We hardly dared set foot on the ground beneath which the dead were sleeping. With short, cautious steps we followed the great black bird who marked out a path among the epitaphs and tombstones. We walked so lightly our shoes scarcely bent the yellow grass. We feared the accident that had befallen the village drunkard.

Believing in his drunken state that he was going into the auberge, the drunkard had walked into the graveyard one November night, cursing and blaspheming. God wanted to punish him. He guided the man towards an old grave whose cover had rotted. The drunkard's foot sank into it, the dead man grabbed his ankle and took the drunkard's toes between his pointed teeth. The drunkard was so afraid that night, he stopped drinking!

Everyone knew this story, which our parents had told us, and that was why we walked so lightly in the graveyard.

We returned every evening in November, to pray for the dead. The church was just beside the graveyard; we would run back home, often with our eyes shut. Once night had fallen, the village belonged to the dead. We couldn't doubt it and you'd have thought the same if you'd heard the story of Madame Zanna: she was trembling and pale as she told it to my father.

One night Madame Zanna heard a noise above her head, in the ceiling. She awakened her husband and they turned on the lights. Nothing. But the noise didn't stop. It sounded like a dog gnawing on a bone. They didn't have a dog. "It's the month of the dead," the husband thought suddenly. They leaped out of bed and, suffocating with fear, they prayed for the souls of the dead. Gradually the noise diminished, then stopped completely. They were so afraid they couldn't get back to sleep. Trembling with cold and fear, they waited for the day. Light chases ghosts away. When it was noon Madame Zanna and her husband, armed with rosaries and holy water and accompanied by neighbours, finally had the courage to go up to the attic where the demonic noise had come from, up above their bed. They found a bone. A bone that looked like a human bone. Our parents had seen that bone. We went to church and prayed on November nights because we wanted to keep the souls of the dead from getting out of their coffins to go and beg for prayers.

We also knew the story of Père Grégoire. He was, as they said, a village boy who'd become a missionary. He used to write letters from Africa in which he told how he chased away the devil so God could enter the hearts of the little pagans. Then the letters stopped coming. Several months later his parents learned that he had disappeared in the bush, probably to be martyred and then devoured by some pagan tribe. A few years later, only the old people remembered Père Grégoire. One night in the month of the dead the curé was awakened by loud organ music. He jumped out of bed, wrapped his coat around him and ran to the church, where he was surprised to see all the windows lighted as though by bright sunlight. He opened the door: the church was full, full of kneeling Africans. At the altar, the priest officiating over this unbelievable mass turned around to say: "Peace be with you." The curé recognized Père Grégoire. The curé was so surprised that he fainted. Next morning he was found stretched out on a bench, dazed, like a man who is intoxicated and smells of alcohol.

Around mid-November the wind became aggressive; it clutched at the roofs of our houses, it pounded against the walls; at night, the walls cracked, the beams and floors creaked. To us, these sounds were caused by the souls of the dead. We were sure of it because on the walls of our bedrooms, on November nights, we could see their fingers, long fingers, as long as the branches of trees.

"November ghosts, where are you now?"

In Montreal, on rue Sainte-Catherine, they don't answer me.
They no longer come to frighten children.

Do the ghosts no longer believe in the living?

SON OF A SMALLER HERO

WAR HELD SWAY over the earth: "the greatest conflict in the history of mankind," it said in *L'Action catholique*. Never had so many men done battle; never had men borne such powerful weapons; and never had men died in such great multitudes. And never had those who were not at the front been so well informed about what was happening in the war. You had only to put your ear against the big radio to hear the voice of the war as you might have heard people quarrelling on the other side of a wall.

The war sowed havoc in our village too. If you wanted to get butter at the general store — or meat or sugar — the law required you to supply a prescribed number of coupons. Onésime, behind the counter, his patience tried by this requirement, grumbled as he crammed coupons into his pocket.

"Oh! life won't be so complicated when this war's over!"

Boys from the village had been called up, as they said, and sent far away, to Europe, to the countries at war. On Sunday at mass we'd hear their mothers sniffle when the curé asked the good Lord to "protect from the fires of Hell their souls, whose lives are in far greater danger than their bodies." When we came out of church my friend Lapin and I, listening to the local gossip, would sometimes hear: "Pray for them, sure, but not too hard, or they'll come back too soon and start drinking like pigs again and singing shameful songs that make your ears blush!"

The strong arms of the war had come to collect the sons of the village and its hideous face came to haunt my father's garage. Never will I forget the poster that faced the enlarged photograph of Monsieur Duplessis on the wall opposite: on it was drawn a group of uniformed officers; they stood so stiff they seemed to be dressed in steel; they wore tall caps with a swastika on them. And they wore rows of coloured medals. Their faces looked like death's heads. All carried revolvers whose barrels, tragic crowns, rested against the shaven head of an emaciated child — who wore a star. (My unshakable conviction that war is a way for adults to persecute children was, no doubt, sown there.) I wished I could help the child flee from the hands of his macabre executioners. But I was only a child myself.

From time to time a truck came to collect scrap iron. My father explained to me:

"They'll melt the scrap iron in a factory, just like your mother melts sugar when she's making jam. The iron turns liquid and clear as water. Then they pour it into moulds to make hulls for boats, and tanks and bombs."

To help the war effort, people gave the truck any old iron that was lying around in their barns and attics: pieces of pipe, old bed-springs, rusty nails, horseshoes, buckets with holes in them, nicked scythes . . . Lapin and I went exploring in the rock piles, those long rows of stones heaped up in the fields where the farmers would leave tools and implements they couldn't use or repair, abandoning them to rust. With all the generosity of our young strength, we wanted to help make tanks and cannons and shells to destroy the people who were torturing the little boy on the poster. If we scraped our hands on the rusty metal, or saw a drop of blood, we were filled with pride like war heroes.

And then one day our house was invaded by toothpaste. A flood! The man who carted goods between the train station and the village unloaded dozens of crates of toothpaste at our house. We piled them in the cupboards and behind the drapes, we hid them behind the sideboard and under the beds. My father had carried off another of his deals! My mother was doubtful but my father was convincing.

"That toothpaste cost me nothing. And I'll sell it for twice as much."

"Two times nothing," my mother retorted, "is still nothing."

She had been a schoolteacher.

It wasn't easy to sell toothpaste to the farmers.

"My horse," said one of them, "he never used that stuff in his life and he's got two rows of choppers that look better than your plate."

The women seemed interested. They knew instinctively that beauty requires loving care, but at the very moment they were about to buy, their husbands would interrupt:

"Woman! don't waste your money on soapsuds when there's a war on. After it's over, then we'll see."

My father had promised me that in a few days the house would be free of the clutter of cases of toothpaste because he would have sold them all. But his customers hardly helped him keep his promise.

One evening the truck that collected old metal for the war stopped in front of our house.

"If your tubes of toothpaste didn't cost you anything," said my mother, "why don't you just get rid of them?"

(In those days toothpaste tubes were made of soft lead.) My father started. He thought for a moment then, smiling, almost triumphant, he said:

"When you're holding onto a fortune you don't throw it away, you help it grow."

The next day he decided I was to accompany him on one of his trips. It would be a fine day, he told me, because I'd learn something from it. He'd prepared his sales pitch in his head. I listened to him talk to the customers.

"Bonjour, lovely lady. I hope everything's all right with you, aside from the World War. It's sad when you think of it: here we are, all quiet and peaceful, and over there on the other side, in Europe, folks are killing each other off . . . A sad thing it is. Doesn't matter if the enemy falls, but our side . . . our own children . . . Mustn't let them get killed, eh lady? Gotta help them defend themselves. Can't send guns in the royal mail, but, you know, if everybody sent a little metal, just an empty tube of toothpaste say . . . Lovely lady, there'd be enough lead for cannons, bombs, tanks . . . Now if I'm wrong there, you tell me . . ."

I listened to my father in the evening too, after supper, out on the gallery that went around the house. The men from the village came there to smoke and chat and rock in their chairs with him. He'd describe the tanks he'd seen pictures of in *L'Action catholique*, he'd describe them as though he'd been born in one. (I listened, my mother sighed.)

"Now you see how deep the foundation of this house is: broad as your two arms spread wide open. Now the sides of a tank are just as thick. Our soldiers are safe inside them . . . No bullet's gonna get through that. Even the good Lord, he'd have a hard time getting through. But I hear the army's short of tanks . . . Oui Monsieur . . . The folks on this side, at peace, aren't sending over enough lead . . . Now if everybody gave a hand and sent a little lead — well, our soldiers'd be saved; it's drops that make an ocean. If everybody just sent one empty tube of toothpaste . . ."

He was silent then, smoking and dreaming. The men with him smoked and dreamed as well.

A few days later there were no more cases of toothpaste in the house.

When the war was over the children from the village who hadn't been killed returned to the fold. A party was organized to celebrate the victory and their homecoming. One of the veterans invited my father to take part.

"Why sure, I'm gonna go and celebrate with the rest of you," said my father.

"You," said the former soldier, "you sacrificed yourself for us from one end of the country to the other . . ."

"That's the truth," said my father. "You notice what nice white teeth the women got?"

PIERRETTE'S BUMPS

EVER SINCE we'd started school Pierrette was the tallest girl in our class, the one who sat in the last row at the back, the one who was always last when we marched through the village in order of height, accompanied by two nuns as the wind tried to pull away their veils. Pierrette was a quiet girl; she didn't really attract our attention except when, in a sentence during reading or an example in grammar, the word "big" appeared; then all heads would turn in her direction and the classroom would be filled with noisy chortling; Pierrette would blush and be silent. Aside from that, Pierrette was like the rest of us, just another student; and that was why I wondered, when Pierrette walked by, why the big boys would stop yelling, put down their ball and stop to look at her.

One evening the men from the village were sitting with my father on the wooden gallery. Words rose in the air with the smoke from their pipes, words as dark as the night that was drawing near. They talked about how life was going badly in the world. But they declared they were happy there was a leader like Duplessis to protect Quebec. I listened, a child in their midst, fascinated by all that these men knew.

"I'm scared about the future," said one of them. "Duplessis won't be around forever, like the good Lord. And what'll happen to us when we haven't got Duplessis any more?"

Suddenly they were silent. They stopped smoking. Pierrette was walking along the sidewalk. Not talking, not smoking, they examined her. My father too.

"Watch out, Pierrette," one of the men called, "you're gonna lose them."

The others guffawed and slapped their thighs with their big workers' hands, bent over and shaken by their laughter. Pierrette walked faster, to escape.

"Papa," I asked, "what's Pierrette going to lose?"

Hearing me, the men were paralysed, as though struck by lightning.

"This is men's talk," my father stammered, blushing.

The others, coming to his rescue, began to explain why it was that without Duplessis, "they'd've never got electricity in the stables."

I left the group of men. Just what was Pierrette going to lose? I was far more obsessed by this question than by the future of Quebec or the politics of Duplessis. It prevented me from sleeping.

In the schoolyard the next day, I approached the territory reserved by the big boys for playing ball. A few minutes later, Pierrette appeared. The big boys broke off their game as though the ball had become a heavy stone. Their eyes followed Pierrette as though she were the Pope. It was time to take action.

"Watch out, Pierrette," I shouted, "you're gonna lose them."

Pierrette fled, taking refuge in the school. One of the big boys picked up the ball and said to me majestically:

"Don't get in a sweat, kid, they won't fall off, they're fastened on good and solid. I checked myself."

The ball began to fly from one boy to the other, joyously, amid bursts of laughter. I decided then to laugh louder than all the big boys. But I still didn't know what it was that Pierrette was going to lose, and what was so firmly fastened on.

For days my glance followed Pierrette; I invented all sorts of tricks to uncover her secret. I spied on her from behind an open book, I brought a little mirror that I used so I could see behind me, I hid under the stairs Pierrette would walk down. But Pierrette still looked as she always did, timid, plump, blushing and the biggest girl in our class. The big boys could have explained to me but I didn't dare display my ignorance, I was so afraid of their mockery.

One morning, to celebrate a religious holiday, our whole class was taken to the church. All in a row, by order of height, we went to take Communion. But scarcely had we returned to school when the nun curtly ordered Pierrette to stand up. Blushing, Pierrette obeyed.

"Instead of displaying such languorous, sensual postures in front of the men in our parish," the indignant nun roared, "you'd be better off praying to God, Pierrette, to chase the evil thoughts from your possessed body. When a person has such provocative bumps on her body it's because the Devil's within you."

Pierrette's face became even redder, then it suddenly turned white; she swayed and crumpled to the floor.

"You see," said the nun, "the Devil is leaving her body."

When I approached Pierrette, who had fallen to the yellow floor when she fainted, I didn't see the Devil but I noticed what I'd never noticed before: Pierrette's chest was puffed out just like a real woman's. But why couldn't the big boys go on playing ball when they saw her?

I hesitated for a long time before confiding in my friend Lapin.

"Pierrette fainted today because the Devil put bumps on her body. Two big bumps, right here!"

"Come on!" said Lapin, "it wasn't the Devil that did that."

My friend Lapin was doubly superior to me: he was older and his father worked in the office of Duplessis' government in Quebec. I understood what his profession was when, after school, behind the big rock we used as a secret hiding place, my friend Lapin opened a paper bag as I watched him.

"This comes from my father's office."

He took out a dozen magazines that had nothing but photographs of girls on every page, girls with no clothes on; and all of them were possessed by the Devil because they had bumps! Bigger bumps than Pierrette. The magazines burned my hands like fire, but I was hungry to learn! I wanted to know! On every page I turned I could feel the sea of ignorance retreating. At every picture my body ceased to be that of a child and I became a man.

"These magazines come from the United States," said Lapin.

"I'd like that, to live in the United States," I said, slowly turning the pages.

I discovered that the United States was a truly amazing country because they knew how to print such beautiful magazines, while in Quebec the newspapers only knew how to take pictures of Cardinal Villeneuve or Maurice Duplessis in his old hat.

"In the United States," Lapin explained, "the streets are full of girls like that!"

"There can't be many Catholics in that country," I said.

"In the Protestant religion there's no such thing as sin."

As I couldn't leave for the United States immediately to become a Protestant, I went back to school the next day as usual. That morning, I played ball with the others. When Pierrette came into the schoolyard I put the ball on the ground and watched her go past with the same expression in my eyes as the big boys.

WHEN THE TAXES SPLIT THE ROOF

NEW BROTHERS and sisters kept arriving endlessly; we had to enlarge our house. With vulgar words that burned our children's souls, the workmen scraped the cedar shingles off our house, knocked down the walls and blocked up the windows; beside new wood, hundred-year-old planks awoke from their sleep. It smelled good, like the forest, as though sap had travelled between the grooves joining the old wood to the new.

Then came the day when the workmen took off the roof. We were asleep in our beds at the usual hour, as we were every night. Our beds were in their proper places but our ceiling was the starry sky. Although our mother had taken from the chest woollen blankets, which, in wintertime, protected us from the threats of strong winds, we shivered as though we were about to sprout wings. Never had we seen the sky so vast. At times I had to clutch my blankets so I wouldn't topple into the enormous well. We had learned in school that there are more stars in the sky than there are flowers on earth. Each golden dot in the depths of the sky was billions of millions times bigger than I. Beneath the sky I was a grain of dust that the slightest wind could have swept away; my hands clung to the blankets. Everything was good again. I listened to the good Lord breathing in His heaven. Why had He not given the children wings so they could soar from one star to another? Once again my bed seemed unstable, drifting on the blue water of the night; and again I clutched the sheets. Around me my brothers laughed dryly, like those who have little fear in their throats. I fell asleep. For me, the sky was a tranquil roof.

In the morning I woke up, bigger now because of the immensity of the sky. Never would I forget that when you live on earth you also live beneath the sky. Even now, man seems not to have been made of the earth under his feet but to have sprung from the sky above his head. It would be impossible for me to see myself in any other way than as a grain of dust lost on the crust of the sky.

We were dislodged from the sky by the workmen with their planks and nails, their saws and hammers. Downstairs in the kitchen, my father and mother were sitting at the big table. We jostled one another as we shouted, telling of our great adventure. Neither my father nor mother looked up. Their faces were marked with despair. Had they been crying? They didn't speak or move, they were bent down. On the table a letter lay unfolded.

"Defraud the government . . ." my father moaned.

"Defraud the government . . ." my mother repeated.

"Defraud," said my father again. "I never learned how to do that."

My father was accused by the government of not paying all the taxes that he owed it. The government was demanding the unpaid balance, under the pain of a fine. My father wanted to pay that very morning. For him, a man wasn't a man if he couldn't pay cash.

He thought, too, that a man isn't a man if he doesn't put a roof over his children's heads. Before we were born he went far away, behind the mountains, in search of money that would make him able to build a house like the one in the dream to which he often abandoned himself as he sat at the window, smoking. On Sundays he would select a volume, always the same one, from a series of books filled with pictures of far-off countries. He never read, but from page to page travelled to those countries where snow-storms didn't exist. One day, he stopped before a Greek temple: "Wife," he said, "that looks like the house I'm going to build you some day." Later we would often see him open the book and, sur-rounded by the smoke from his pipe, spend long hours dreaming of the Greek temple.

When he had accumulated the necessary money, my father went to see the contractor, carrying the book under his arm. They spent the day arguing before the book, opened to the page with the Greek temple.

"Defraud the government," said my mother, "as though we weren't honest."

"Defraud — I don't even know what it means . . ."

We were on the stairs, bewildered by our parents' despond-ency, and we were silent. Suddenly my father rushed outside, furi-ous. Never had anyone in the village seen him in a hurry. But that morning he ran, and people still remember it.

The contractor had just arrived to begin his day's work. My father stood, arms spread open, in front of the rusty, dented truck, which stopped with a squealing of its old brakes.

"I'm stopping the work!" my father shouted. "I'm stopping everything!"

The contractor burst out laughing. My father was famous for the funny stories he brought back from the other side of the mountains (and which he never told in the house); for the con-tractor, this joke about interrupting the work when he hadn't yet put the roof on the house was really very comical.

"You'll have the only house without a roof in the whole county! Makes sense, though: you won't have to shovel off the snow in the winter!"

The contractor's face was red from laughing.

"I'm stopping the work!"

My father was shouting so hard there were tears in his eyes. The women had come out on the galleries, lingering there as they pretended to be busy. The contractor, seeing my father cry, didn't dare believe it was a joke. He silenced the motor of his truck. My father got in and sat beside him.

Through the windshield, where the sun was reflected in the dust and mud, you could see only the two men's shadows. The children dared not come any closer and the women gradually went back inside the houses.

Then my father got out of the truck, which rattled, shook, turned around and went sheepishly back up the hill. My father came and took his place at the table where my mother waited for him, in front of the letter from the government. They didn't speak to each other.

A few minutes later the contractor walked into the house: timidly, without saying hello, without looking at my father or mother, he placed a fat envelope on the table, then left as he had come in. My father's fingers, stained brown by tobacco, tore open the envelope and took out some banknotes in different colours, which he pushed towards my mother. She counted them carefully, almost piously.

"Now then," my father ordered, "you're gonna write to the Tax Government in Ottawa and tell them, around here we know more about paying than defrauding."

Meanwhile, the workers dismantled the scaffolding, tossing the pieces into the contractor's old truck.

"Walls without a roof . . ." they grumbled.

". . . it's like a man without a head."

September nights aren't as warm as July. The villagers paraded past our house, trying to see without looking.

My father immediately prepared to drive his black Ford to the other side of the mountains. Along came the bank manager: he'd been told of our misfortune. He hastened to offer his help. My father answered him curtly:

"A man that takes other people's money is a thief. I'm going to put the roof on my house with money I earn from my own work, by the sweat of my brow. Thanks very much."

"I didn't want to hurt you. Even the good Lord borrowed. He borrowed a mother ..."

"Not from your bank."

My father got into his car.

Through the windows of our rooms without ceilings, without a roof, we gazed at the Ford as it raised a cloud of dust on the gravel road which appeared, then disappeared, depending on the hills and trees. My father had said:

"I'll be back with the roof."

"What if it rains?" my mother asked. "The children ..."

"A little rain never hurt anything that's growing!"

That night, lying under the roof of the vast night, I didn't dream that I was flying like a bird. A great anxiety threw my child's heart into turmoil. Was it the anxiety of all who question the night, yet know nothing of it, understand nothing?

THE HOCKEY SWEATER

THE WINTERS of my childhood were long, long seasons. We lived in three places — the school, the church and the skating-rink — but our real life was on the skating-rink. Real battles were won on the skating-rink. Real strength appeared on the skating-rink. The real leaders showed themselves on the skating-rink. School was a sort of punishment. Parents always want to punish children and school is their most natural way of punishing us. However, school was also a quiet place where we could prepare for the next hockey game, lay out our next strategies. As for church, we found there the tranquillity of God: there we forgot school and dreamed about the next hockey game. Through our daydreams it might happen that we would recite a prayer: we would ask God to help us play as well as Maurice Richard.

We all wore the same uniform as he, the red, white and blue uniform of the Montreal Canadiens, the best hockey team in the world; we all combed our hair in the same style as Maurice Richard, and to keep it in place we used a sort of glue — a great deal of glue. We laced our skates like Maurice Richard, we taped our sticks like Maurice Richard. We cut all his pictures out of the papers. Truly, we knew everything about him.

On the ice, when the referee blew his whistle the two teams would rush at the puck; we were five Maurice Richards taking it away from five other Maurice Richards; we were ten players, all of us wearing with the same blazing enthusiasm the uniform of the Montreal Canadiens. On our backs, we all wore the famous number 9.

One day, my Montreal Canadiens sweater had become too small; then it got torn and had holes in it. My mother said: "If you wear that old sweater people are going to think we're poor!" Then she did what she did whenever we needed new clothes. She started to leaf through the catalogue the Eaton company sent us in the mail every year. My mother was proud. She didn't want to buy our clothes at the general store; the only things that were good enough for us were the latest styles from Eaton's catalogue. My mother didn't like the order forms included with the catalogue; they were written in English and she didn't understand a word of it. To order my hockey sweater, she did as she usually did; she took out her writing paper and wrote in her gentle schoolteacher's hand: "Cher Monsieur Eaton, Would you be kind enough to send me a Canadiens' sweater for my son who is ten years old and a little too tall for his age and Docteur Robitaille thinks he's a little too thin? I'm sending you three dollars and please send me what's left if there's anything left. I hope your wrapping will be better than last time."

Monsieur Eaton was quick to answer my mother's letter. Two weeks later we received the sweater. That day I had one of the greatest disappointments of my life! I would even say that on that day I experienced a very great sorrow. Instead of the red, white and blue Montreal Canadiens sweater, Monsieur Eaton had sent us a blue and white sweater with a maple leaf on the front — the sweater of the Toronto Maple Leafs. I'd always worn the red, white and blue Montreal Canadiens sweater; all my friends wore the red, white and blue sweater; never had anyone in my village ever worn the Toronto sweater, never had we even seen a Toronto Maple Leafs sweater. Besides, the Toronto team was regularly trounced by the triumphant Canadiens. With tears in my eyes, I found the strength to say:

"I'll never wear that uniform."

"My boy, first you're going to try it on! If you make up your mind about things before you try, my boy, you won't go very far in this life."

My mother had pulled the blue and white Toronto Maple Leafs sweater over my shoulders and already my arms were inside the sleeves. She pulled the sweater down and carefully smoothed all the creases in the abominable maple leaf on which, right in the middle of my chest, were written the words "Toronto Maple Leafs." I wept.

"I'll never wear it."

"Why not? This sweater fits you . . . like a glove."

"Maurice Richard would never put it on his back."

"You aren't Maurice Richard. Anyway, it isn't what's on your back that counts, it's what you've got inside your head."

"You'll never put it in my head to wear a Toronto Maple Leafs sweater."

My mother sighed in despair and explained to me:

"If you don't keep this sweater which fits you perfectly I'll have to write to Monsieur Eaton and explain that you don't want to wear the Toronto sweater. Monsieur Eaton's an *Anglais*; he'll be insulted because he likes the Maple Leafs. And if he's insulted do you think he'll be in a hurry to answer us? Spring will be here and you won't have played a single game, just because you didn't want to wear that perfectly nice blue sweater."

So I was obliged to wear the Maple Leafs sweater. When I arrived on the rink, all the Maurice Richards in red, white and blue came up, one by one, to take a look. When the referee blew his whistle I went to take my usual position. The captain came and warned me I'd be better to stay on the forward line. A few minutes later the second line was called; I jumped onto the ice. The Maple Leafs sweater weighed on my shoulders like a mountain. The captain came and told me to wait; he'd need me later, on defense. By the third period I still hadn't played; one of the defensemen was hit in the nose with a stick and it was bleeding. I jumped on the ice: my moment had come! The referee blew his whistle; he gave me a penalty. He claimed I'd jumped on the ice when there were already five players. That was too much! It was unfair! It was persecution! It was because of my blue sweater! I struck my stick against the ice so hard it broke. Relieved, I bent down to pick up the debris. As I straightened up I saw the young vicar, on skates, before me.

"My child," he said, "just because you're wearing a new Toronto Maple Leafs sweater unlike the others, it doesn't mean you're going to make the laws around here. A proper young man doesn't lose his temper. Now take off your skates and go to the church and ask God to forgive you."

Wearing my Maple Leafs sweater I went to the church, where I prayed to God; I asked him to send, as quickly as possible, moths that would eat up my Toronto Maple Leafs sweater.

FOXES NEED FRESH WATER

THEY USED TO tell us that rich ladies in the big cities wouldn't buy fur coats unless they were made from our foxes. These rich ladies thought our foxes had a "sheen" the rest of the foxes in the world were deprived of. So our foxes were reserved from birth for the coats of some rich lady or other. The breeders would often make fun of them as they threw carrion to the animals: "there you go, a shovelful of guts for the fat lady." A fox is a fox, after all, and why would the good Lord make our foxes finer than anyone else's?

As the men waited for winter to end they would talk about these things, smoking their pipes. Monsieur Josaphat said:

"Me, I think the reason our fur's better looking than anywhere else is because of the water we give our foxes."

His firm belief triggered off some laughter, but the men sucked on their pipes and put all their mockery into their expressions. Monsieur Josaphat, disturbed by his own opinion, was taken aback for a moment; he felt himself turn pale and it made him furious. Those who hadn't dared to laugh before, roared now.

Monsieur Josaphat was the biggest fox breeder, the one with the largest number of grilled cages: when people heard the captive beasts howl at night they used to say: "It's Monsieur Josaphat's foxes again." Our mothers prayed that the animals wouldn't escape from their cages, for there were always some children around. The other main breeder, Ferdinand Chapeau, didn't have quite as many cages, but every year he built new ones and bought new mothers. It was his ambition that one day Monsieur Josaphat would sell out to him and he'd become the only breeder.

Monsieur Josaphat's foxes and Ferdinand Chapeau's foxes drank the same water. Their cages were set up on adjoining plots of land. In the middle, between the cages, a natural basin was always filled with fresh water, summer and winter. All year round, Monsieur Josaphat's foxes, and Ferdinand Chapeau's, enjoyed the best water. The villagers were in the habit of saying that the water they drank wasn't as tasty as the foxes': "If you want proof," one wag said, opening his shirt, "my hair hasn't got the same sheen as the foxes'!" Monsieur Josaphat and Ferdinand Chapeau came in turn to the basin, with two horses pulling a sleigh made of big pieces of pegged cedar; they would fill two or three barrels with the precious water, return to their cages and empty the barrels into wooden troughs. The foxes would cry out with pleasure and smile sinister smiles.

In those days, Monsieur Josaphat thought the water was useful only to quench the foxes' thirst; he still hadn't understood that it contained a magic ingredient that made the foxes' fur shimmer like the soft brilliance of the water. But then, all at once, he understood: an inspiration. Now he could no longer doubt. How could he have raised foxes for so many years without knowing that the splendour of their fur came from his water? His water was truly a precious possession.

For several years he had allowed Ferdinand Chapeau to dip water from his basin — not out of generosity, but ignorance. This water, with its miraculous qualities for the foxes' fur, belonged to him. This water had beautified Ferdinand Chapeau's furs for years, and Ferdinand Chapeau had never given him anything in return. He would never give him anything. Ferdinand Chapeau had offered to buy all the scraps from the butcher; if the butcher agreed, Monsieur Josaphat would have been forced to buy food for his foxes in the next village, or even farther. That's the kind of man Ferdinand Chapeau was, whom all these years Monsieur Josaphat had so generously supplied with water. Thanks to this water, received with never any payment, Ferdinand Chapeau strutted about, flattering himself that he had the finest foxes in the village. Ferdinand Chapeau was prospering. Hadn't he already boasted that he'd soon be able to buy Monsieur Josaphat's business? But what would Ferdinand Chapeau have been without his water?

That day when he went, as was his custom, to fill his barrels at the basin, Ferdinand Chapeau was bowled over by what he saw: a fence around the basin. On it was a notice: "It is strictly forbidden to take any of this private water under pain of a lawyer's letter payable by the receiver. Signed: The Proprietor."

In vain did Ferdinand Chapeau trace lines, find guide marks, boundary-lines beneath the snow, recall that his father's horses and his grandfather's had drunk water from Monsieur Josaphat's basin; in vain did he read and reread notarized documents and government forms. His fate was sealed: the water belonged to Monsieur Josaphat's land.

A farmer from the other end of the village who had too many children and who had gone into debt at the village tavern, allowed Ferdinand Chapeau to persuade him to sell his water. In the days that followed you would see his two horses pulling the sleigh and the three barrels down the village street; he didn't look up. The angry man whipped his animals relentlessly. The children heard him mutter words they didn't dare repeat to their parents.

None of the villagers understood Monsieur Josaphat's deci-
sion. He had to explain: "There's nobody got the right to harvest
your oats, there's nobody got the right to take your horse, there's
nobody got the right to take your wife; and there's nobody got the
right to take your water." Sometimes, when he knew Ferdinand
Chapeau had gone in search of water, Monsieur Josaphat would
come up to his cages. It seemed to him that the fur of Ferdinand
Chapeau's foxes was losing its lustre.

Then it was spring. The air grew warm, the foxes demanded
more water. Monsieur Josaphat added a padlock to the little gate
that opened onto the spring. Once again Ferdinand Chapeau stud-
ied the limits, the boundaries, he noted the line of the fence, analyzed the conditions attached to the possession of the lots from
the earliest days. There was no possible doubt: Monsieur Josaphat
was unattackable.

By June the land had absorbed the springtime water. For
Ferdinand Chapeau it was time to look for a spring for his own
property. For several days he had been searching for a discreet
bubbling of water on the surface, a water hole that wouldn't
be a muddy swamp. Suddenly, among the rocks, he discovered
a trickle running through the moss: the water was so cold it
cut your fingers. This living water was just as fine as Monsieur
Josaphat's. To be so pure this water had to run — but where? It disappeared immediately, creeping beneath the ground. And where
did it go? Ferdinand Chapeau examined the conformation of the
land. Beneath the knolls, water — Ferdinand Chapeau's water —
and its underground current flowed, quivering and fresh, rushing
towards Monsieur Josaphat's basin.

Very early next morning, with great discretion, Ferdinand
Chapeau went back to his spring, carrying a pick, a shovel and
a bag of cement. When Monsieur Josaphat went to his basin to
fill his barrels, the water was no longer flowing. The basin was

draining. The day after, the earth at the bottom of the basin began to crack, it was so dry. The foxes were thirsty.

The farmer from the other end of the village who had too many children and had gone into debt at the village tavern agreed to sell water to Monsieur Josaphat. He paid more for it than Ferdinand Chapeau, a "faithful, long-standing customer," the farmer insisted.

During the summer, Monsieur Josaphat and Ferdinand Chapeau, with their horses, their two-wheeled carts and their barrels, met from time to time; they didn't see each other.

"After his own blood," Monsieur Josaphat explained when he went to the general store, "the most precious thing a man's got is his water. You mustn't waste it by giving it to just anybody."

At the general store Ferdinand Chapeau was very careful not to gloat.

"The good Lord's always told men to share; Josaphat refused to share so he's been punished with drought. If he showed a little generosity maybe by some miracle the water'd start to pour out of his spring again."

Monsieur Josaphat didn't feel like being generous and Ferdinand Chapeau was too honourable to return the water to a man who refused to share it.

It was a dry summer, drier than anyone had seen for years. The grass burned; the leaves wrinkled on the trees. The man who had too many children and had gone into debt at the tavern noticed, between drinking sprees, that the two fox-breeders were drying up his well. They found him at the well one morning, shotgun in hand. That day the foxes went without water. You could hear them moan.

"I know where there's some water," said Ferdinand Chapeau at the general store.

His words were carried back to Monsieur Josaphat, who replied:

"I'd rather have an empty basin than a basin full of water Ferdinand Chapeau found."

In the fall, the buyers from the large factories came in their big cars and went away without buying any furs. In November after the heavy frost, people learned that Monsieur Josaphat's foxes, and Ferdinand Chapeau's, had to be killed; they'd caught some disease from drinking bad water.

The grilled cages were silent but the pungent odour of foxes persisted after the first snow. Monsieur Josaphat and Ferdinand Chapeau undertook to dismantle the cages before the first big storms. To avoid seeing each other, they turned their backs as they worked.

One morning, the water came back to Monsieur Josaphat's basin. It melted the snow.

When Ferdinand Chapeau saw this catastrophe he swore he wouldn't wait for spring to throw stones and cement into Monsieur Josaphat's water.

A GREAT HUNTER

WHEN HUNTERS TOLD how they had taken the animal by surprise or how its own foolishness had led it to them, you had only to see the fire in their mouths or eyes to know that killing brought them a great deal of joy.

I liked Louis Grands-pieds' stories. He would never tell any more. That day, we were taking him to the graveyard. My friend Lapin, carrying the censer, and I the holy water, very dignified in our black soutanes and starched lace surplices, were leading the cortège to the site the sacristan had shown us.

For years Louis Grands-pieds had been suffering from an incurable disease. He rarely got up before noon. All day he would drag behind him the weight of his bed. No one dared reproach him for his laziness; a man's entitled to be sad and stooped and tired.

But when the hunting season came! Then Louis would get up long before the sun, he would dress in wool and jump in his car which had wings as it sped through the sleeping villages along a gravel road all curves and humps and bumps. In the dark, when the yellowed grass began to be visible — very pale because of fog and the grey light — Louis got out of his car, walked around to

the other side and opened the door as though for a lady. He took
out his rifle.

Softly, without singing, without catching his clothes on the
branches, he walked into the forest filled with night. The path was
so familiar he could have walked its whole length with his eyes
closed. Near the end the ground was softer. Through his rubber
boots he could feel moss; the lake was near. He recognized the
smell of water mingled with that of the night. Every autumn morning for several years Louis Grands-pieds came that way. Before he
spied the lake he took a sip of brandy. As he was walking beneath
the branches, day had approached in the sky. The lake exhaled
white steam like that which came from Louis' mouth. This was
the lake where animals came to drink. He had seen beaver swim
from one stump to another. Sometimes he had seen hoofprints,
moose or deer. Every morning, Louis Grands-pieds was sorry
he had come so late. "The moose came to drink in the middle
of the night," he thought, looking for a stump that had taken on
the shape of a chair, with a back, when the tree was felled. It was
Louis' custom to sit there and wait for the game that would certainly
come to drink one day. No one else knew this refuge.

He drank a little brandy. He had discovered this place when
he was a child and he always came back to it. The sun was climbing higher in the sky, he could see it through the leaves whose
bright colours were awakening. There was a splash in the water.
A frog. There were thousands in the lake. Louis had laid his rifle
on the moss near the stump. He picked up his flask of brandy to
fan within him a delicious fire that would drive away the cold of
this autumn morning. Another frog jumped in the water. Then a
branch broke. Another frog! This one jumped into the branches!
Louis Grands-pieds looked up. Twenty feet from him, its head and
antlers surrounded by dry leaves, a moose watched Louis with an
old man's eyes. Louis was paralysed. Then, instead of picking up

his rifle, Louis Grands-pieds had only one thought: to offer his flask of brandy to this animal with the sad eyes. Instead, he did what a hunter is born to do. He picked up his rifle and fired. The morning shattered like a crystal glass. Had Louis closed his eyes before he fired? When he heard the shot he knew he didn't want to kill the moose, this living, breathing animal, he didn't want to put to death this head with the expression that was so human. The animal fled. Louis swallowed some brandy. He climbed up on the stump and looked at the place where he had seen the moose. The water in the lake seemed like a smooth mirror between the stumps and submerged tree trunks. Louis drank some brandy. Gradually, reflections tinted the quiet water a darker hue.

Why did Louis Grands-pieds not want to kill his moose? He was too good. He had been a good child, he had never pulled cats' whiskers, he had never torn the legs off flies, he had never made a toad smoke a cigarette, he had never stepped on a flower. Louis was too good; he was caught in his goodness like a butterfly in its cocoon. It was the cocoon that had kept him from firing. Every autumn the other men in the village paraded with their deer and their moose exhibited on their cars. Louis had scarcely dared to look at the animal. If he had fired at the moose it was to make it run away.

Louis drained the flask of brandy. Sitting on his stump, in this place filled with perfumes and silence, he decided he would stop being good. He swore he would kill the moose.

Every morning that autumn until the snow was deep, he returned to the place to watch and wait, rifle in hand. As autumn advanced he came earlier and earlier to the lake where the moose must return to drink. Winter spread out its fine crystalline layer. And the moose remained invisible.

Louis Grands-pieds' incurable illness overcame him, but neither the white blizzards of February nor the July sun could erase from his memory the image of the big moose he hadn't killed because he was too good.

The next autumn, on the first day of the hunting season, Louis got up long before dawn. He drove through the familiar villages that the night erased completely from the mountains, he followed the little gravel road and found again the path to the lake. Louis walked like a hunter whose bullet would strike his victim in the heart. It was still night, dark. Soon the light would awaken. In the first ray of dawn the animals would come out to drink fresh water.

Louis walked. The night seemed to breathe against his ear like a tracked beast.

Louis forced himself to learn not to be good. He drank some brandy. In the clearing. His chair-shaped stump was in its place, grey, amid the high brown grass. He sat, drank some brandy. On this morning which must resemble the first morning God had made for man, Louis despised his goodness. When the moose came he would fire.

Close to the pond there was a crumpling of dry leaves. Branches cracked. The moose.

Louis Grands-pieds shoulders his rifle.
He is too good. He hates his goodness.
Louis Grands-pieds will kill this moose another day.
The moose laps at the clear water.
Louis Grands-pieds places his rifle on the moss.
He swallows some brandy.

On the pebble road leading to the graveyard, in a silence that put a lump in your throat, I heard Louis Grands-pieds' drawling voice tell his story, as he had done so many times. My friend Lapin had heard it too, because he whispered:

"If Louis Grands-pieds couldn't ever shoot a moose, how come he could put a bullet through his own head?"

The curé, who was carrying the cross in the procession, ordered us through the words of his Latin prayer:

"Be quiet, and show some respect for the dead!"

I remember that grey day very well; it was a day when we said nothing more at all.

WHAT LANGUAGE DO BEARS SPEAK?

FOLLOWING OUR OWN morning ritual, to which we submitted with more conviction than to the one of saying our prayers when we jumped out of bed, we ran to the windows and lingered there, silent and contemplative, for long moments. Meanwhile, in the kitchen, our mother was becoming impatient, for we were late. She was always afraid we'd be late . . . Life was there all around us and above us, vibrant and luminous, filled with trees; it offered us fields of daisies and it led to hills that concealed great mysteries.

The story of that morning begins with some posters. During the night, posters had been put up on the wooden poles that supported the hydro wires.

"Posters! They've put up posters!"

Did they announce that hairy wrestlers were coming? Far West singers? Strong men who could carry horses on their shoulders? Comic artists who had "made all America collapse with laughter"? An international tap-dance champion? A sword swallower? Posters! Perhaps we'd be allowed to go and see a play on the stage of the parish hall — if the curé declared from the pulpit that the play wasn't immoral and if we were resourceful enough to earn the money for a ticket. Posters! The artists in the photographs would gradually come down from the posters until they inhabited our dreams, haunted our games and accompanied us, invisible, on our expeditions.

"There's posters up!"

We weren't allowed to run to the posters and, trembling, read their marvellous messages; it was contrary to maternal law to set foot outside before we had washed and combed our hair. After submitting to this painful obligation we were able to learn that we would see, in flesh and blood, the unsurpassable Dr. Schultz, former hunter in Africa, former director of zoos in the countries of Europe, former lion-tamer, former elephant-hunter and former free-style wrestling champion in Germany, Austria and the United Kingdom, in an unbelievable, unsurpassable show — "almost unimaginable." Dr. Schultz would present dogs that could balance on balls, rabbit-clowns, educated monkeys, hens that could add and subtract; in addition, Dr. Schultz would brave a savage bear in an uneven wrestling match "between the fierce forces of nature and the cunning of human intelligence, of which the outcome might be fatal for one of the protagonists."

We had seen bears before, but dead ones, with mouths bleeding, teeth gleaming. Hunters liked to tell how their victims had appeared to them: "... standing up, practically walking like a man, but a big man, hairy like a bear; and then it came at me roaring like thunder when it's far away behind the sky, with claws like knives at the end of his paws, and then when I fired it didn't move any more than if a mosquito'd got into its fur. Wasn't till the tenth bullet that I saw him fall down ..." Loggers, too, had spotted bears and some, so they said, had been so frightened their hair had turned white.

Dr. Schultz was going to risk his life before our eyes by pitting himself against this merciless beast. We would see with our own eyes, alive before us, not only a bear but a man fighting a bear. We'd see all of that!

A voice that reached the entire village, a voice that was magnified by loudspeakers, announced that the great day had arrived: "At last you can see, in person, the unsurpassable Dr. Schultz, the man with the most scars in the world, and his bear — a bear that gets fiercer and fiercer as the season for love comes closer!" We saw an old yellow bus drive up, covered with stars painted in red, pulling a trailer on whose sides we could read: DR. SCHULTZ AND ASSOCIATES UNIVERSAL WONDER CIRCUS LTD. The whole thing was covered with iron bars that were tangled and crossed and knotted and padlocked. A net of clinking chains added to the security. Between messages, crackling music made curtains open at the windows and drew the children outdoors. Then the magical procession entered the lot where we played ball in the summer. The motor growled, the bus moved forward, back, hesitated. At last it found its place and the motor was silent. A man got out of the bus. He stood on the running-board; twenty or thirty children had followed the circus. He considered us with a smile.

"Hi, kids," he said.

He added something else, words in the same language, which we'd never heard before.

"Either he's talking bear," said my friend Lapin, "or he's talking English."

"If we can't understand him," I concluded, "it must be English."

The man on the running-board was still talking; in his strange language he seemed to be asking questions. Not understanding, we listened, stupefied to see Dr. Schultz in person, alive, come down from the posters.

"We talk French here," one of us shouted.

Smiling again, Dr. Schultz said something else we didn't understand.

"We should go get Monsieur Rancourt," I suggested.

Monsieur Rancourt had gone to Europe to fight in the First World War and he'd had to learn English so he could follow the soldiers in his army. I ran to get Monsieur Rancourt. Panting behind his big belly, he hurried as fast as he could. He was looking forward to speaking this language. He hadn't spoken it for so many years he wasn't sure, he told me, that he could remember it. As soon as he saw the man from the circus he told me: "I'm gonna try to tell him hello in English."

"Good day sir! How you like it here today?" ("I remember!" Monsieur Rancourt rejoiced, shouting with delight. "I didn't forget!")

Dr. Schultz moved towards Monsieur Rancourt, holding out his hand. A hand wearing a leather glove, in the middle of summer.

"It's because of the bear bites," my friend Lapin explained to me.

"Apparently the *Anglais* can't take the cold," said one of our friends whose mother's sister had a cousin who worked in an *Anglais* house in Ontario.

The man from the circus and Monsieur Rancourt were talking like two old friends meeting after a number of years. They even laughed. In English, Monsieur Rancourt laughed in a special way, "a real English laugh," we judged, whispering. In French, Monsieur Rancourt never laughed; he was surly. We listened to them, mouths agape. This English language which we'd heard on the radio, in the spaces between the French stations when we turned the tuning knob, we were hearing now for real, in life, in our village, spoken by two men standing in the sun. I made an observation: instead of speaking normally, as in French, instead of spitting the words outside their lips, the two men were swallowing them. My friend Lapin had noticed the same thing, for he said:

"Sounds like they're choking."

Suddenly something was overturned in the trailer; we could hear chains clinking, a bump swelled out the canvas covering and we saw a black ball burst out — the head of a bear.

Dr. Schultz and Monsieur Rancourt had rolled up their shirt-sleeves and they were comparing tattoos.

"The bear's loose!"

The animal ran out on the canvas, came down from the roof of the bus and jumped to the ground. How could we tell that to Dr. Schultz who didn't understand our language, whose back was turned to the trailer and who was completely absorbed in his conversation?

"Monsieur Rancourt!" I shouted. "The bear's running away!"

There was no need to translate. The man from the circus had understood. Waving a revolver, he sped towards the bear, which was fleeing into a neighbouring field. He shouted, pleaded, threatened.

"What's he saying?" we asked Monsieur Rancourt.

"Words that English children don't learn till they're men."

"He must be saying the same words my father says when a cow jumps over the fence. They aren't nice."

Dr. Schultz, whom we had seen disappear into the oats, came back after a long moment and spoke to Monsieur Rancourt, who ran to the village. The men who were gathered at the general store rushed off to find other men; they took out traps, rifles, ropes. While the mothers gathered up their children who were scattered over the village, the men set out, directed by fat Monsieur Rancourt. Because of his experience in the war, he took charge of the round-up. Dr. Schultz had confided to him, we learned later:

"That bear's more important than my own wife."

They mustn't kill it, then, but bring it back alive.

The show was to begin in the early afternoon. Dr. Schultz, who had gone with the men into the forest, came back muttering; we guessed that he was unhappy. At his trailer he opened the padlock, unfastened the crossed iron bars, pulled out the pegs and undid the chains. We saw him transform his trailer into a stage, with the help of a system of pulleys, ropes and tripods. Suddenly we were working with the circus man: we carried boxes, held out ropes, unrolled canvas, stuck pickets in the ground, lined up chairs. Dr. Schultz directed our labours. Small, over-excited men that we were, we had forgotten he was speaking a language we didn't understand.

A piece of unrolled canvas suspended from a rope, which was held in place by stakes, formed a circular enclosure. It resembled a tent without a roof; we had built it. We were proud; would we, as long as we lived, ever have another day as beautiful as this one? From now on we were part of the circus.

At last it was time for the show. The music cried out as far as the horizon. In the stands there were mostly women: the men were still pursuing the lost bear.

In gleaming leather boots, in a costume sparkling with gilt braid, Dr. Schultz walked out on the stage. He said a few words and the crowd applauded fervently; the spectators no doubt considered it a mark of prowess to speak with such ease a language of which they couldn't utter a single word.

He opened a cage and a dozen rabbits came out. On the back of each he hung a number. At the other end of the platform was a board with holes cut out of it. Above each hole, a number. The man from the circus gave an order and the rabbits ran to the holes that bore their numbers. Unbelievable, wasn't it? We all raised rabbits, but our animals had never learned anything more intelligent than how to chew clover. Our hands were burning, so much had we applauded our friend Dr. Schultz. Next came the trained dogs' act: one danced a waltz; another rode around a track on a bicycle while his twin played a drum. We applauded our great friend hard enough to break our metacarpals.

The acrobatic chimpanzee's act had scarcely begun when a great uproar drowned the music from the loudspeakers. The canvas wall shook, it opened, and we saw the captured bear come in. The men from the village were returning it to its master, roaring, furious, screaming, clawing, kicking, gasping, famished. The men from the village, accustomed to recalcitrant bulls and horses, were leading it with strong authority; they had passed ropes around its neck and paws so the furious animal had to obey. Monsieur Rancourt was speaking French and English all at once.

When he saw his bear, Dr. Schultz let out a cry that Monsieur Rancourt didn't translate. The men's hands dropped the ropes: the bear was free. He didn't notice immediately. We heard his harsh breathing, and his master's too. The hour had come: we were going to see the greatest circus attraction in the Americas, we were going to see with our own eyes the famous Dr. Schultz, our friend, wrestle a giant black bear.

No longer feeling the ropes burning its neck, no longer submitting to the strength of the men who were tearing it apart, the bear stood up, spread its arms and shot forward with a roar. The bear struck Dr. Schultz like a mountain that might have rolled onto him. The bear and our friend tumbled off the stage. There was a ripple of applause; all the men together would never have succeeded in mustering half the daring of Dr. Schultz. The bear got up again, trampled on the great tamer of wild beasts and dived into the canvas enclosure, tearing it with one swipe of its claws before disappearing.

Dr. Schultz had lost his jacket and trousers. His body was streaked with red scratches. He was weeping.

"If I understand right," said Monsieur Rancourt, "he's telling us that the bear wasn't *his* bear . . ."

"It isn't *his* bear . . ."

The men shook and spluttered with laughter as they did at the general store when one of them told a funny story.

The men laughed so hard that Monsieur Rancourt could no longer hear Dr. Schultz's moans as he lay bleeding on the platform. The undertaker apologized for the misunderstanding.

"That bear was a bear that talked English, though, because I didn't understand a single word he said."

INDUSTRY IN OUR VILLAGE

ONE DAY, on the train that joined my village to Quebec City, a man in farmer's clothes was sitting across from a very dapper-looking man who smelled of money. Both men were smoking: one his thick pipe, the other a long cigar. The route was long and tortuous. After a few minutes in the smoke, the man from my village ventured to say to the man with the jewels:

"You must come from the big city, Monsieur."

"Yes," said the other man curtly, "but not you!"

"Me, I come from Sainte-Justine."

"Ah! I don't know that place," said the shining man. "You must admit, it's not as well known as Montreal." And he added, "There must be more cows than people in your population!"

The man from my village felt these words like a slap. He was silent as he smoked his pipe and prepared his revenge. When he was ready he emerged from his silence and his smoke, saying:

"Yup, it's a little village, but Sainte-Justine's pretty famous because of the factory."

The man from my village began to smoke his pipe again; the trap had been set.

"What kind of factory?" the city man inquired at last.

"A shirt factory," said the man from my village.

"It can't be very big."

"Maybe it ain't as big as some," said the man from my village, "but every day this train, this train right here, has to bring us buttons."

The man from the city, not understanding, deigned to smile.

"You can count," said the man from my village, clutching his pipe; "this here train's got fifteen cars; there's one for people like you and me and the other fourteen, they're for the buttons for our shirt factory. And the same train comes back every day."

Hearing this story or telling it consoled the people from my village somewhat for having to live in an area that had more spruce trees than smokestacks. One day a villager came close to changing that situation.

Monsieur Juste was a blacksmith by trade, but horseshoes were no longer a sufficiently broad field for him; he dreamed of business, of firms, he dreamed of big chimneys spitting black smoke. When the joke about the carloads of buttons was told in his presence, Monsieur Juste would say that if they wanted, it could stop being a joke and become reality.

"There's no reason," he said, "why the products from our village shouldn't be sold in every store from Halifax to Vancouver."

Monsieur Juste, perceptively, had observed for some time that during milking the cow's tail swings to the left and right, sometimes slapping the farmer in the face, which is unpleasant. He had also observed that the animals' hind feet were constantly twitching and sometimes kicking out, which puts the pail of milk in great danger of being overturned. It was a serious problem. Monsieur Juste searched through several catalogues of farm products, he leafed through his collection of the *Bulletin des Agriculteurs*, he even went and looked in the curé's encyclopedia, but he found nothing. He came to the conclusion that never before had mankind thought of solving the problem of the restless legs and tails of cows. Monsieur Juste reflected for a few weeks; with his thick blacksmith's pencil he made many drawings on his bags of chewing tobacco. Once the bag was empty he would throw it out, always forgetting his drawings, and begin again. Then one day he found it! His dream, his idea, his project — now he could begin to create it in iron.

Bent over his anvil, he twisted the iron into the shape of a hook, into large manacles that would be fitted to the cow's hocks. Such a hook would be placed on each of the animal's legs. Between the hooks, Monsieur Juste arranged an adjustable chain that could hold the recalcitrant limbs firm and motionless. To this chain Monsieur Juste welded a smaller one, whose purpose was to hold the swinging tail in place. A great problem, then, had been solved: it was, no doubt, a step backwards for the cows, but a great leap forward for mankind.

Monsieur Juste made a few of these devices but when he suggested them to the farmers in the village they simply laughed in his face. Monsieur Juste didn't grow discouraged; he had read in magazines about the lives of great inventors; he knew these great men were always misunderstood by those around them. He decided, then, to turn to the world outside.

With his wife, he wrote a letter describing his invention, praising its usefulness. His letter ended with these words: "In the modern era one cannot live without the invention of Monsieur Juste." Then he had the letter translated into English by the postmaster: in fact, Monsieur Rancourt had learned English in the army during the First World War. And that was how Monsieur Juste's invention was given the English name "Anti-Cow-Kicks!"

Madame Juste carefully wrapped her husband's invention in tissue paper, folded the letter translated into English and attached it to the chain; she placed the precious object in a box, carefully wrapped the box and, as the postmaster had told her, she wrote: "From Juste Industries Ltd., Sainte-Justine, Canada. To the I-Don't-Know-What Company, Texas, U.S.A." Monsieur Juste had noticed the address in one of his farm magazines.

Monsieur Juste waited. His shop grew silent. The hammer no longer struck the anvil. Monsieur Juste did not work. He spent days beside the fire, sitting on the anvil, telling how the idea had come to him of dealing with the United States.

"If you want to be successful in business," he would say, "you have to dive in horns first, like a bull. The money's there in front of you! Now us French Canadians, we're afraid of money. But I'm gonna prove to you that I can be successful."

A month later, a letter arrived from Texas. Monsieur Juste, trembling, asked the Postmaster to translate it for him. The I-Don't-Know-What Company in Texas was buying Monsieur Juste's invention; it was ordering 2,500 dozen Anti-Cow-Kicks!

Monsieur Juste had hardly arrived back home when the fire began to roar in his forge. The hammer began to strike the anvil again, feverish amid Monsieur Juste's shouts of joy. It was late at night and the hammer was still striking the anvil. Then it was silent for a few hours until, long before the birds began to sing, the hammer started ringing out again. On Sunday the shop was silent, but the hammer struck the anvil at the same time the clock struck midnight.

After seven days of strenuous labour, Monsieur Juste had made seven dozen Anti-Cow-Kicks. The company in Texas had ordered 2,500 dozen! Monsieur Juste put down his hammer.

"I'm ruined," he said.

PERHAPS THE TREES
DO TRAVEL

THERE WERE THOSE who had travelled like migratory birds and those who lived rooted to the earth, like trees. Some had gone very far. I remember hearing the story of a man who had gone to the place where the sky meets the earth: he'd had to bend down so he wouldn't bump his head against the sky. The man had suddenly felt lonely and he'd written to his wife. The stamp cost a thousand dollars. Some people had gone to New York; another visited a brother in Montana; my grandfather had sailed on the Atlantic Ocean; a family had migrated to Saskatchewan; and men went to cut timber in the forests of Maine or Abitibi. When these people came home in their new clothes, even the trees on the main street were a little envious of the travellers.

And there were those who had never gone away. Like old Herménégilde. He was so old he'd seen the first house being built in our village. He was old, but his mustache was still completely black. It was a huge mustache that hid his nose, his mouth and his chin. I can still see old Herménégilde's mustache like a big black cloud over our village. Our parents used to say of him that he was healthy as a horse; all the storms of life had been unable to bend his upright, solid pride. At the end of his life he possessed nothing but a small frame house. All his children were gone. Old Herménégilde had spent his whole life without ever going outside the village limits. And he was very proud of having lived that way, rooted to the soil of our village. To indicate the full extent of his pride he would say:

"I've lived my whole life and never needed strangers!"

Old Herménégilde had never gone running off to the distant forests, he had never gone to the neighbouring villages to buy or sell animals. He'd found his wife in the village. Old Herménégilde used to say:

"The good Lord gave us everything we need to get by right here in our village! How come people have to go running off somewheres else where it ain't no better?"

He recalled a proverb written by a very old French poet and repeated it in his own way:

"The fellow next door's grass always looks a heck of a lot greener than your own."

Old Herménégilde had never been inside an automobile.

"I'm in no rush to die," he said. "I want to do it on foot, like a man."

One morning a black car longer than the one driven by Monsieur Cassidy, the undertaker, stopped with a jolt in front of old Herménégilde's house. A son he hadn't seen for a good many years got out of the car, all dressed in black, as Monsieur Cassidy usually was.

"You coming to my burial, my boy?" asked old Herménégilde.

"No," said the son. "I came to take you on a trip."

Moving from one trade, one job to another, the son had become the private chauffeur to a businessman from Montreal; before he could ask himself what was happening, old Herménégilde, who had never been in a car before, was pushed onto the leather seat of a Cadillac that pawed the ground like a horse.

"Father," said the son, "you can't die before you see the world a little."

"I've seen everything a man needs to see," said old Herménégilde.

The son's long black car carried him off at a speed he'd never experienced. To avoid seeing that he was going beyond the village limits, old Herménégilde closed his eyes. And with his eyes closed the old man didn't see that he was driving through the neighbouring village, where a number of old men had gone to get their wives; he didn't see Mont Orignal, the highest mountain in the region; he didn't see the ten villages the black car drove through at a speed no runaway horse had ever reached. Tobie, his son, was talking, but he didn't want to listen.

"I'm your son and I know you've spent your whole life as if you were in jail. But you gotta see the world before you die and I'm the one that'll take you out of that jail. Nowadays there's no such thing as distance. My boss, he gets up in Montreal, he opens his eyes in Toronto, he eats his breakfast in New York and then comes back to Montreal to go to sleep. That's what I call living! You gotta keep up with the times. We know the world turns. And you gotta turn with it. I never stop travelling. I know the world. I know life. But you, you've never lived in modern times. It's something you gotta see."

"A man can go as far as he wants," said old Herménégilde, "but he always stays in the same pair of boots."

"I'm not what you'd call a good son," said Tobie, "but I'm the one that's gonna show you the world. That'll be one good thing I've done in my life."

So then old Herménégilde understood that he was no longer allowed to keep his eyes closed. They had entered Quebec City. In a single glance the old man took in houses taller than the church, more people in the street than for a religious procession and cars swarming everywhere, like ants. His son drove him in front of an immense château, a real château whose name he'd heard when people talked about the rich — the Château Frontenac; then he showed him something much older than he was, older even than his late father — the houses built by the first Frenchmen.

The black car stopped in front of a large garden. Tobie helped his father get out.

"Now people won't be able to say you died without ever setting foot on the Plains of Abraham. This is where we lost our country . . ."

And then it was time to go home. In the car, the son noticed the old Herménégilde was keeping his eyes closed.

"Father, don't shut your eyes, look at the people."

"I seen too much," said the old man, "you showed me too many things today."

As soon as the son had left old Herménégilde at his house, he hurried off again in the long black car, summoned by other journeys in the vast modern world.

For long months, behind his big black mustache and his closed eyes, old Herménégilde waited for the long black car to return.

THE GOOD PEOPLE AND
THE BAD PEOPLE

I WAS VERY YOUNG the day I discovered the truth. It was during the war. (The Second World War had no other name.) The truth told us the world would be paradise if it weren't for the bad people. All the misfortunes in our village and all the misfortunes in the Old Countries were caused by the bad people.

The war came to an end. The very bad people were conquered. It seemed that happiness was going to return to the earth, just as I asked God in my prayers. All that would be left then would be to take care of the not-so-bad people. I had an uncle who'd become a priest to convert the bad people; I assured God that I was prepared to become a priest too. I was nine years old. Peace seemed to be a good thing.

One man protected this peace and happiness in the land of Quebec — a man not like other men, a man who knew how to help the good people and how to be feared by the bad. My father had tacked up a photograph of our premier in his garage: I looked at it often. The man was sitting down, a battered broad-brimmed hat on his head, an old habitant's hat, while before him paraded children to whom he was handing out money. What a generous man he was! I decided it was better to be like Duplessis — le chef

— than my uncle the priest. From the mountain I looked around at the other villages, also built on mountains; I looked at the church steeples, the gravel roads, the green trees, the small rivers — and I was happy because no one would come and violate all this beauty as long as Duplessis was there to protect us.

All the Nazis had most likely been put in prison; that was why we heard nothing more about them. But other bad people, very bad people had hypocritically used trickery to rise up and try to dominate the good people; they threatened the happiness of the good people. These were the Communists. Once more, because of the bad people the good people wouldn't be able to sleep without anxiety.

The Communists were beginning to take over the Old Countries. In our village, the curé explained why. Because the Old Countries had abandoned the true religion — ours, that is — they were being punished with a fatal disease: Communism. We in Quebec had continued to practise the true religion reverently; we had continued to pray to the real God. So why were the Communists threatening us? Why were they infiltrating groups of workers who no longer wanted to obey their bosses? Why were the Communists trying to poison us with pamphlets, with letters that told lies about the true religion? Happily, Duplessis was protecting us; he sent a number of Communists to prison and he didn't hesitate to put padlocks, for years, on the doors behind which Communists held meetings to perfect their plan for the domination of Quebec.

At suppertime my parents talked about an article in the newspaper. The good people's newspaper was called *L'Action catholique*. That evening I read the article, an editorial (I learned the word that evening). The journalist heaped abuse on the Communists. Never in the village during quarrels had I heard so many insults. The good people had the right to insult the bad, ten times more so if the bad people happened to be Communists. I still remember the conclusion of the article: "the Catholics of Quebec will stand erect in the face of the horde of Communist invaders; we will fight proudly to the last drop of our blood." I felt I could see Stalin in Moscow, furious, grumbling into his mustache, humiliated by the article in *L'Action catholique* from Quebec. To fight the bad people I announced that it was better to be, not like Duplessis, but rather like the intrepid journalist who had dared defy the Communists' top leader, Stalin himself.

In my village there were good people and bad people, but there were no Communists. In the autumn I was sent away to a little seminary to learn Latin; I found no Communists there either. When I whispered to my confessor that I wanted to defend the good people against the Communists he blessed me three times, then wrote an address on a bit of paper and took a few coins from the pocket of his soutane so I could subscribe to a magazine that would teach me all a man might want to know about Communism. It was written by a Jesuit missionary who had spent years as a prisoner in Russia and by another man who had been a Communist agent in Canada and then repented and became a policeman. After a few issues there was nothing I didn't know. I was ready to attack Communists like the journalist from *L'Action catholique*, whose style I copied in my own writing. Then I announced to my friends at the seminary that the Communist danger was greater than we knew, that Communists had infiltrated the factory at the bottom of the hill where they spun wool, and all the factories in Quebec — and even the government. It was impossible to see but it was present, gnawing away like a cancer. Communism had perhaps even attacked some priests. I named names, cited facts I'd read in my magazine. I wrote by hand an anti-Communist newspaper that I circulated in my class. We had to be vigilant. I even made speeches in the club devoted to developing our oratorical gifts — passionate speeches denouncing in no uncertain terms the spies in the pay of Moscow. I still, however, had not seen any Communists. Not a single one. Sometimes we were given permission to walk in the town of Saint-Georges-de-Beauce, in a long line of uniformed seminarians. If I spotted a man who seemed to look a little morose I couldn't help thinking he must be a Communist. Quebec could feel secure: Duplessis and I, with all the strength of my twelve years, wouldn't give up the struggle of truth against lies.

But as I would soon learn, the truth I possessed was not complete. I received a paper in the mail read by "only those who don't fear the truth," a little newspaper with big ambitions that in four pages told the whole truth about the real evils in our society. The newspaper dazzled me; at last it shed light on the true face of the really bad people. I had to subscribe to it. The paper told me that the great ills of the world are caused by the banks, the factories and business. And who owned the banks, the factories, business? The Jews. It took three or four issues to convince me. I even wrote to the editor of the paper: the Communists, I objected, were more dangerous than the Jews. He replied that Communism was a disguise the Jews hid behind as they prepared to take over the world. "Don't you know that Karl Marx, the father of Communism, was a Jew? And if you look at Stalin's picture aren't you convinced that he has a Jewish nose?" The editor had written the letter himself, with a pen. How could I still doubt? I remained perplexed for several days, then I received another issue of his paper. On the front page, a headline: "Proof of the International Jewish Plot"; under it, a photograph of the three masters of the world: Roosevelt, Stalin and Churchill. The three statesmen were shaking hands and their crossed arms formed a sort of triangle that the editor had circled with black ink. Beneath it, this note: "this triangle, one of the essential symbolic figures of the Talmud, is proof that the traitors are unmasked." I didn't exactly understand the editor's learned language, but I could only be convinced.

I hadn't managed to see any Communists in Saint-Georges-de-Beauce but there were some Jews. One had a clothing store on Deuxième Avenue. I persuaded my friend Lapin to come and take a close look at the enemy of the entire world. Trembling, we walked into the little shop: the ceiling was low; articles of clothing were jumbled on a large table, suits were hanging on the walls and others were suspended from long tubes attached to the ceiling.

"What do you want?" asked a man who appeared amidst the suits, with an accent that didn't come from the Beauce.

I couldn't tell him I'd come to contemplate the enemy; I was trembling, but deep down I knew that I was brave. I dreamed up a lie:

"We came for a suit."

"Take whatever you want, for you today, half-price!"

My friend Lapin looked around, felt the cloth, compared the colours. (He didn't want a suit.)

"That one," said the Jew with his strange accent, "you'd look real smart in it. I don't sell schmattas here."

The Jew handed him the jacket.

"A jacket for that price they don't make any more. And today, for the seminarians, I don't charge you the tax."

Lapin looked at himself in a mirror on the door, a yellowed mirror, then said to me:

"Give me two bucks, I want to leave a down-payment. It's a bargain!"

Back at the seminary I reread the little paper that told all the great truths, then I lent it to Lapin, asking him to read in particular an article entitled "Buy from French Canadians, not from agents of the international Jewish plot."

Next day, my friend Lapin asked me if I'd go into town with him; together we went to return the jacket to the Jewish store-keeper on Deuxième Avenue. When we walked out of the disturbing shop after receiving our refund, my friend Lapin and I were dazzled for a moment by the bright light of May, already as beautiful as summer holidays. We had just gallantly brought down an enemy, but at thirteen we still had many more battles against many other enemies before us, until the good people triumphed over the bad.

DO MEDALS FLOAT ON THE OCEAN?

NO GENERAL, not even the most intrepid, is decorated with the number of medals worn by the Catholic child I once was. They hung in a cluster about my neck, bringing together most of the saints in Heaven. They were at my service: one protected me against the flu, another against impurity; one would help me find lost objects, another to regret my sins; one would be with me at the hour of my death, another would help me obey my parents. The saints suspended about my neck were ambassadors too, who reported to God my words, my actions and my slightest thoughts.

The bouquet of medals gradually became a weight around my neck. One evening I threw them up towards Heaven, one by one. They didn't fall down to earth; that was the explanation I gave the overseer of my school who made me hunt in the fields, on my knees, for the medals I had profaned by tossing them around like pebbles.

Several years later, I was leaving for France where I would spend several years. This journey troubled my mother. France was so far away and I was leaving with so little money. France was a country without religion and I had so little. I was going for so long — what would happen to her grown-up child? She didn't want to let me go without protection. That was why, in the middle of the Atlantic, when the sky was low and the waves were churning furiously, I found, sewn into the lining of my jacket, a sheaf of medals.

"Chère maman!"

How concerned she must have been about my fate, to have, without my knowledge, sewn these medals inside my jacket! I went into my cabin and wrote: "Chère maman, You sewed so many medals inside my jacket that our boat's listing to the side I'm standing on . . ." I felt no desire to throw the medals into the raging sea.

Clinging fast to the guardrail so I could resist the powerful wind, and dizzy before the watery abysses that opened, closed and collided, I thought of a story I had heard. It overwhelmed me, for it was the first time I'd heard anyone doubt the value of the medals we all wore around our necks.

In the summer my father used to sit on the gallery that went around the house, facing the setting sun. The men who went by, at loose ends after their day at work, would stop to have a smoke with him. I listened with the ears of an astonished child to the remarks of these men who knew so many things that I was ignorant of. That was where I heard the story I remembered on the freighter tossed about on a stormy sea between Quebec and France, between adolescence and manhood. I thought of the men from my village sitting with my father, smoking. One of them said:

"In this life two things are important: arithmetic and catechism."

The other replied:

"In modern life nowadays I think you oughtta know more arithmetic than catechism."

My father added:

"Too much arithmetic and not enough catechism doesn't make for a good life."

Then Monsieur Veilleux said:

"Us French Canadians, we know the catechism better than anybody in the world. But are we the richest or the happiest?"

Monsieur Veilleux's words carried a lot of weight; he had travelled to several cities in Quebec and even to Ontario; his experience was broader than that of the others: he had seen the world.

"Man," Monsieur Veilleux went on, "has to know arithmetic better than anything else. Because arithmetic's education."

One of the men protested:

"If everybody's got an education the land'll be covered with priests and lawyers and notaries and doctors. Then who'll grow the carrots and potatoes?"

Monsieur Veilleux replied:

"I'll give you proof that education's better than religion. Now you take two men: one of them's got an education, always going around with a pencil in his pocket. The other man, all he knows is his catechism; so he hasn't got no pencil in his pocket but he's got a load of medals around his neck. Now let's just say these two men, one with a pencil and the other one with the medals, they fall down a well. Both of them land at the bottom. The medals too. But that pencil's gonna come up to the surface and float. And when you see that pencil floating you're gonna say: 'Arthur fell down the well.' And you'll go and rescue him. Now Albert, he's gonna stay at the bottom, with his medals. So there's your proof that a pencil's worth more than medals and education's worth more than religion."

After this story my father and his friends smoked for a long time, saying nothing, while before their eyes the sun rolled behind the mountain.

Looking at the sea that was deeper than the well in Monsieur Veilleux's story, I mechanically put my hand in my jacket pocket to check whether I had a pencil. If all the saints on the medals my mother had sewn inside my jacket were powerless, from now on I could count on my pencil.

GRANDFATHER'S FEAR

GRANDFATHER WAS A strong man. Grandfather liked physical strength. His entire life had been a hand-to-hand combat, a test of strength. Grandfather knew only what he had conquered through the strength of his arms. When he was young, almost a child, he was a lumberjack; as a young man he already had children; in the midst of the great frozen silence he could hear them crying off in the distance, in his little frame house. Then he would tackle the giant spruce trees, striking with all his muscles tense, battling the hard wood; and the forest would move back. I've seen a photograph of him from that period: among the other lumberjacks, with his face of an adolescent turned prematurely old, he was as proud as a king. I look at his eyes; because I am his grandson I know: he's thinking that he's the strongest.

Grandfather felled so many trees he was able to buy a farm. In his fields there were more rocks than earth. Grandfather took them away one by one, before he could plant. In the winter the frost would bring more rocks to the surface and every spring he would take up the struggle again. Then he planted. Grandfather didn't swear like the other farmers; he smiled, because he was the strongest.

A few years later, Grandfather became a blacksmith. I've seen him fighting with the red-hot iron, I've seen him sweating, his face black, surrounded by sparks, battling with the iron — which he always succeeded in bending. He was the strongest. His strength was quiet, like the strength of a maple tree. I had spent so many days of my childhood with him that he no longer knew if I was his son or his grandson, but he always told me as he crushed my writer's hand in his own enormous one:

"That (he meant his strength), that's something you don't learn in books."

His big hand would finally open to free my numb fingers and I said:

"Being as strong as you are, you must be afraid of nothing."

"Fear," Grandfather replied, "that's something I've never known in my life."

"Him, not been afraid?" my grandmother asked ironically, in one of her outbursts of laughter. "I can tell you, I remember when he was scared of Protestants."

Grandfather got abruptly to his feet.

"If I don't put on some wood my fire's gonna go out."

And closing the door he grumbled:

"Fear, that's something I never knew."

Grandmother took great pleasure in revealing Grandfather's secret to me. She told me the story of Grandfather's fear.

As a young girl, Grandmother had lived in Sainte-Claire. My Grandfather lived thirty miles away, in the mountains at Sainte-Justine. In order to visit his fiancée, Grandfather took a long road, winding with detours, hills and bumps. The mud lay thick on it. It climbed up hills, then came back down dangerously, avoiding stones and stumps. Between the two villages a few houses were grouped around a small church. Protestants lived in these houses. The small wooden church was a Protestant church. It was a Protestant village.

Grandfather, as strong as the forest, as strong as the rocks in the fields and as strong as iron, was never able to overcome his fear of passing through the Protestant village. As soon as he spotted it he would jump out of his carriage, seize the horse's bridle and take a detour through the trees. When he'd passed the village he would get back on the road that led him to his fiancée.

Grandmother, who had just betrayed a secret, laughed like a schoolgirl suddenly grown old during the joke. I felt myself becoming sad.

Who, I wonder, could have planted such a great fear in the soul of a man who was so strong?

THE SORCERER

IN THE EVENING the bus came back from town. Sometimes it would stop and we'd watch a child from the village, as they used to say, who'd been away for a long time, get off with his suitcases and look around as though he had arrived in a foreign place.

The village was built on the side of a hill. Because of the difference in levels, we could lie in the grass on the slope and have our eyes at street level. Discreetly spreading the blades of grass, we could see without being seen. We could spy on life.

One evening the bus stopped in front of us. The powerful brakes gripped the steel of the wheels and made them shriek. The door opened and we saw shoes covered with grey spats on which broad striped trousers fell; the man placed his foot, in its spat, on the pavement and emerged from the shadows inside the bus. He was wearing a top hat like the magicians who came to put on shows. His coat with tails, as we called his jacket, came down to his calves. There was a white bow-tie around his neck and he carried a leather case like old Doctor Robitaille. The bus set off again. Only then did we notice that the man's face was black.

Was he some practical joker who'd covered his face with black as we did the day before Lent to fool the grown-ups? We knew that Africa was full of Black people, we knew they had them in the United States and on the trains, but it wasn't possible that a Black man had got on the bus and come to our village.

"Either he isn't a real nigger or he's got the wrong village," I said to my friend Lapin, who was lying flat in the grass like a hunter watching his prey.

"Look how white his teeth are; that's the proof he's a real nigger."

Without moving his feet, his feet in their grey spats, the Black man looked up towards the top of the mountain, then down towards the bottom, contemplating for a moment. With his leather case, his jacket open to the wind, his black fingers pinching the brim of his top hat, he began to walk towards the top of the mountain. Lapin and I waited a bit before coming out of our hiding-place so we wouldn't be seen. Then, from a distance, we followed the Black man. Other people were following him too, but they hid in their houses, behind curtains that closed after he'd gone by. A short distance from the place where he'd got off the bus was La Sandwich Royale, one of our two restaurants. The Black man stopped, looked up towards the top of the mountain, then down towards the bottom and, dragging his feet in their spats he went into La Sandwich Royale. A terrible cry rang out and already the wife of the owner of La Sandwich Royale was hopping onto the street, arms raised, in tears and squealing as loud as the butcher's pigs.

"She's a woman," Lapin explained, "it's normal for her to be scared like that."

"A nigger in the missionaries' magazine and a nigger you see right across from you isn't the same thing."

The frightened woman didn't want to go back by herself to where the Black man was. Lapin and I had approached the window and our noses were pressed to the glass. The Black man was sitting at a table.

"The nigger's waiting," Lapin noted.

Several people had come running at the sound of the panic-stricken woman's cries. Pouce Pardu, who'd been in the war, in the Chaudière Regiment, had done everything a man can do in a lifetime. He said:

"Me, I'm not afraid of Black men."

He went inside. The grown-ups approached the window and, like Lapin and me, they saw Pouce Pardu come up to the Black man, talk to him, laugh, make the Black man smile, sit down with him, give him his hand. We saw the Black man hold the brave man's hand for a long time, hold it open, bring it close to his eyes. The wife of the owner of La Sandwich Royale had stopped screaming but she was still trembling.

Through the window we'd seen Pouce Pardu take back his open hand and offer a banknote to the Black man. The owner's wife was somewhat reassured, because she said:

"I'll go back inside if you'll come with me."

We went in, Lapin and I and the other little boys and the grown-ups who were looking in the window; Pouce Pardu announced:

"That nigger can just look at your hand and tell your future and your past."

"Ask him what he wants to eat," said the wife of the owner of La Sandwich Royale.

Another former soldier, who'd fought the war in Newfoundland and who feared nothing either, said:

"The future, I know: I ain't got one. I'm going to ask the nigger to tell me my past."

We'd seen the Black man bend over the soldier's open palm and whisper. After him, other people ventured to approach the Black man and later that evening cars came from the neighbouring villages, filled with people who'd come to see the Black man and who wanted to learn what lay in the future. Lapin and I no longer called him the Black man, but the Sorcerer. For only a sorcerer can know the future: a sorcerer or God. God, of course, wouldn't be black . . .

The next day Lapin and I, crouching in the grass, saw the Black man reappear; we saw him come down from the mountain with his top hat, his spats and his jacket open to the wind. Lapin and I, flat against the ground, held our breath and watched the sorcerer pass: with his white teeth he was smiling like a true devil. So then Lapin and I had no need to talk to each other in order to understand. We took pebbles from our pockets and threw them at him with all the strength of our small white arms.

Several years later I was in Montreal where I was wearing myself out trying to sell my first pieces of writing. One afternoon I was going to a newspaper to try to sell a story entitled "The Princess and the Fireman," when I noticed, on the other side of the street, a Black man wearing a top hat and grey spats, striped trousers and a tailcoat. I hadn't forgotten the Black man of my childhood. Running through the traffic, I crossed rue Sainte-Catherine. It was the Black man of my childhood, the one we'd thrown stones at because of his black skin, his unusual hat, his ridiculous spats, his strange knowledge; it was the same man, old now, bent over, his hat battered, his hair white, his spats soiled and his leather case worn thin. It was the same man! The white bow-tie was greyish now.

"Monsieur! Monsieur!" I called out. "Will you read my hand?" I asked as I caught up with him.

He put his case on the sidewalk, rested his back against the building. I held out my open hand. He didn't look at me, but bent over to see the lines of my palm. After a minute of absorbed silence he said:

"I can read that there's something you're sorry about."

A SECRET LOST IN
THE WATER

AFTER I STARTED going to school my father scarcely talked any more. I was very intoxicated by the new game of spelling; my father had little skill for it (it was my mother who wrote our letters) and was convinced I was no longer interested in hearing him tell of his adventures during the long weeks when he was far away from the house.

One day, however, he said to me:

"The time's come to show you something."

He asked me to follow him. I walked behind him, not talking, as we had got in the habit of doing. He stopped in the field before a clump of leafy bushes.

"Those are called alders," he said.

"I know."

"You have to learn how to choose," my father pointed out.

I didn't understand. He touched each branch of the bush, one at a time, with religious care.

"You have to choose one that's very fine, a perfect one, like this."

I looked; it seemed exactly like the others.

My father opened his pocket knife and cut the branch he'd selected with pious care. He stripped off the leaves and showed me the branch, which formed a perfect Y.

"You see," he said, "the branch has two arms. Now take one in each hand. And squeeze them."

I did as he asked and took in each hand one fork of the Y, which was thinner than a pencil.

"Close your eyes," my father ordered, "and squeeze a little harder . . . Don't open your eyes! Do you feel anything?"

"The branch is moving!" I exclaimed, astonished.

Beneath my clenched fingers the alder was wriggling like a small, frightened snake. My father saw that I was about to drop it.

"Hang on to it!"

"The branch is squirming," I repeated. "And I hear something that sounds like a river!"

"Open your eyes," my father ordered.

I was stunned, as though he'd awakened me while I was dreaming.

"What does it mean?" I asked my father.

"It means that underneath us, right here, there's a little fresh-water spring. If we dig, we could drink from it. I've just taught you how to find a spring. It's something my own father taught me. It isn't something you learn in school. And it isn't useless: a man can get along without writing and arithmetic, but he can never get along without water."

Much later, I discovered that my father was famous in the region because of what the people called his "gift": before digging a well they always consulted him; they would watch him prospecting the fields or the hills, eyes closed, hands clenched on the fork of an alder bough. Wherever my father stopped, they marked the ground; there they would dig; and from there water would gush forth.

Years passed; I went to other schools, saw other countries, I had children, I wrote some books and my poor father is lying in the earth where so many times he had found fresh water.

One day someone began to make a film about my village and its inhabitants, from whom I've stolen so many of the stories that I tell. With the film crew we went to see a farmer to capture the image of a sad man: his children didn't want to receive the inheritance he'd spent his whole life preparing for them — the finest farm in the area. While the technicians were getting cameras and microphones ready the farmer put his arm around my shoulders, saying:

"I knew your father well."

"Ah! I know. Everybody in the village knows each other ... No one feels like an outsider."

"You know what's under your feet?"

"Hell?" I asked, laughing.

"Under your feet there's a well. Before I dug I called in specialists from the Department of Agriculture; they did research, they analyzed shovelfuls of dirt; and they made a report where they said there wasn't any water on my land. With the family, the animals, the crops, I need water. When I saw that those specialists hadn't found any I thought of your father and I asked him to come over. He didn't want to; I think he was pretty fed up with me because I'd asked those specialists instead of him. But finally he came; he went and cut off a little branch, then he walked around for a while with his eyes shut; he stopped, he listened to something we couldn't hear and then he said to me: 'Dig right here, there's enough water to get your whole flock drunk and drown your specialists besides.' We dug and found water. Fine water that's never heard of pollution."

The film people were ready; they called to me to take my place.

"I'm gonna show you something," said the farmer, keeping me back. "You wait right here."

He disappeared into a shack which he must have used to store things, then came back with a branch which he held out to me.

"I never throw nothing away; I kept the alder branch your father cut to find my water. I don't understand, it hasn't dried out."

Moved as I touched the branch, kept out of I don't know what sense of piety — and which really wasn't dry — I had the feeling that my father was watching me over my shoulder; I closed my eyes and, standing above the spring my father had discovered, I waited for the branch to writhe, I hoped the sound of gushing water would rise to my ears.

The alder stayed motionless in my hands and the water beneath the earth refused to sing.

Somewhere along the roads I'd taken since the village of my childhood I had forgotten my father's knowledge.

"Don't feel sorry," said the man, thinking no doubt of his farm and his childhood; "nowadays fathers can't pass on anything to the next generation."

And he took the alder branch from my hands.